PISCES

Edited by Nikky Lee &
Austin P. Sheehan

THE ZODIAC SERIES

The Zodiac Series is a collection of twelve speculative fiction anthologies, each focusing on one of the Zodiac signs. The anthologies feature short stories and poems inspired by each sign, and retellings of the various myths behind those signs.

Capricorn Aquarius Pisces

Aries Taurus Gemini

Cancer Leo Virgo

Libra Scorpio Sagittarius

The Zodiac Series has been produced by Aussie Speculative Fiction, and each anthology contains a diverse selection of tales by talented writers from Australia and New Zealand.

First published by Deadset Press in 2020.

Second Edition published 2021.

© Deadset Press 2020

All rights reserved.

ISBN: 978-0-6488388-1-4

Cover design Copyright © Alanah Andrews.

Edited by Nikky Lee & Austin P. Sheehan.

Foreword by Sasha Hanton.

I AM PISCES

Zoey Xolton

I am the Fish and my constellation is Pisces.

My tarot card is The Moon; I am a dreamer and an intuitive

soul.

At my best I am compassionate, creative and wise.

At my worst I am fearful, escapist and over emotional.

Fluid and balanced, like my element: Water, mine is a Mutable

sign.

I appreciate solitude, sleep, art and spirituality.

However I dislike cruelty, criticism and bringing up the past.

I am ruled by Neptune, and am guardian to the fourth day of

the week.

My colours are purple and teal.

About the Author:

Zoey Xolton is an Australian Speculative Fiction writer, primarily of Dark Fantasy, Paranormal Romance, and Horror. Her works have appeared in over one-hundred themed anthologies, with more due for publication!

She has recently celebrated the release of her debut short story collection Darkly Ever After. *You can find further details regarding her many publications on her website:* www.zoeyxolton.com*!*

CONTENTS:

FOREWORD

Sasha Hanton

The twelfth and final sign of the zodiac, Pisces, the mutable water sign, is represented by two fish with their tails tied together. Overseen by Neptune and Jupiter, Pisces is one of the three star signs ruled over by two planets.

Pisces mythology has a central tale that appears in both Greek and Syrian mythology. The Greek telling of the story has three different interpretations following the escape of Aphrodite and her son Eros from Mount Olympus during the attack of the monster Typhon.

In one version, two fish lead them to safety—the fish tie their tails together to avoid being thrown apart in the current. In another, they turn into fish and tie their tails together to avoid separation before swimming to safety. And in the third variation, Aphrodite and Eros turn into fish and are led to safety by two fish—the two fish guiding them have their tails tied together so that in the chaos they can't be separated. Either way the result and core details remain the same; two fish who tied their tails together to avoid being separated, and in honour of their action, Zeus placed them in the sky as a constellation.

Syrian mythology has two different versions of the myth for the constellation. The first is the same as the Greek with two fish, known as the Ichthyes, who saved the Goddess Ashtarte by leading her down the river Euphrates. In the second, Ashtarte appears as an egg in the Euphrates, which is then carried to the bank by either two fish or two fishermen. There, doves tend to the egg until it hatches to reveal the Goddess. As a reward the two fish are placed in the sky as the Pisces constellation.

Besides mythological roots, all the constellations of the zodiac have ties to the Major Arcana of the Tarot. Pisces shares a special connection with the 18th card of the Major Arcana, the Moon. This card is depicted as a moon above with a shellfish emerging from a pool of water; a path leads from the water and off into the distance between two towers. A dog and wolf baying at the moon complete the scene. It is a card associated with the subconscious, imagination, dreams, secrets, and one's shadow self.

Fittingly with its relation the Moon card, Pisces is the ruler of the 12th House—the house of privacy and secrets in astrology. The depictions of unity between the two towers, the wolf and the dog, are meant to symbolise the balanced life most people lead, and the path between the towers a symbol of the path we desire in life. Pisces and the Moon's connection is symbolic, the depictions in the card display Pisces nature to always dream of something more. As for the shellfish emerging from the waters in the card, it symbolises coming into consciousness and is linked with a tendency for possession of psychic powers.

Those born between February 19th and March 20th, under the Pisces constellation, are often remarked to be the most compassionate individuals possessing a true sense of understanding.

As with Aquarius and Scorpio, Pisces is ruled by two planets that can cast different influences on an individual, depending on what planetary aspects they lean towards.

Jupiter—named for the Roman God of sky and thunder, whose Greek counterpart is Zeus—is the planet of faith, positivity and optimism. It held the position of ruling planet for Pisces up until the discovery of Neptune in 1846.

The modern ruler of Pisces, the planet Neptune is associated with idealism, spirituality, empathy, and imagination. Named after the Roman counterpart of the Greek God Poseidon, ruler of the ocean, Neptune lends a sense of mysticism to those born under its planetary rule.

As one of the most spiritual and imaginative signs in the zodiac, there is no question the stories within these pages will engage and reveal the seemingly endless depths of Pisces.

About the Author:

Sasha Hanton grew up in the tropics of Darwin, Northern Territory. From a young age, she devoured books and iced coffee, both of which she continues to intake on an almost daily basis. Now living on beautiful Bribie Island in Queensland, her time is split between writing and spoiling her puppy Miley.

Sasha, who has a Bachelor of Journalism from Bond University, has dabbled in the journalistic profession but finds fiction far more fascinating. Her first published work The Short Story Press Collection draws on her love for a diverse range of genres and passion for short stories. Coming from a multicultural background (Eurasian) she aspires to make her writing inclusive for people from all walks of life and to bring a unique blend of eastern and western culture to her writing.

Throughout her life, she has been a lover of history and mythology, and at any time will find some way to worm one or the other into her storytelling. When she's not writing or reading she can be found walking her dog and volunteering. You can keep up with her writing over on www.theshortstorypress.wordpress.com

The Fish and the Water Carrier

Fallacious Rose

She was a Pisces. I was Aquarius.

We didn't believe in all that rubbish.

"No wonder you're so cool," I used to say. "You're like a fish, all cold and slimy."

"No wonder you're an Aquarius," she'd say. "You're so damn weird. And water carriers—what do they do with all those buckets, anyway? It's like, so third world."

And so it went, each slur sillier than the last. We lived in our own world, like a long-running Broadway show in which we acted all the parts. She was Caesar, I Brutus. She was Laurel, I was Hardy. She was cool, I was strange.

In the school quadrangle, with its bolted steel benches and adolescents clustering like grapes, we sat apart. We acted our way through Ancient Greece and Imperial Rome as if we were exploring past lives, laughing. I was always the iconoclast, she the upholder of civic values. An Aquarius, after all, always chooses the wrong shoes.

To those on dry land, the ocean is a mystery. You splash at the edges, guess at the depths. But to us who live there, you're just a shadow on the sun, a pair of waving legs. We were sufficient unto ourselves. We ignored your nets, laughed at your bait. When you asked us, 'What do you talk about, for all those hours!' we said, 'lipstick' and doubled over, sniggering.

To you, our schoolmates—no, not mates, strangers who amused us with their fashion sense and boy-band posters—we must have seemed as eccentric as those spiny whiskered monstrosities that pass by the portholes of submarines. To us, you seemed dull earthlings, confined by your own space, time, and tight jeans: we despised you, a little.

All things end—including friendship. The play is over, the audience files out. When school finished, she got a job, and I got a boyfriend. We began the slow and awkward process of learning how to fit in.

The last time we met, we had nothing to say to each other. She was a fish. I was a water carrier. Turned out that ocean we used to swim in was only an aquarium after all.

About the Author:

I live on a rural property on the south-east coast of NSW, Australia, and write under the pen name Fallacious Rose. My elder sister reckons nobody will take me seriously with a name like that but then, I'm not sure I want them to—at least, not always. My brand is 'eccentric', my genre is 'everything', and the only thing standing between me and a career as a famous singer is . . . that I can't really sing. You can find out more, and download a story or two, at www.fallaciousrose.com.

A Gift for Aphrodite

Aiki Flinthart

I hook my toes beneath a coral-crusted rock; cling to the ocean bottom, so I won't float away. Today is my sixteenth birthday and I sit there in the cold gloom and wish for my father. Just for a moment of his star-eyed attention. An instant to acknowledge me. To show more than infinite indifference. Not his presence, here beneath the sea, for that would unmake the world. And I don't hate it enough for that.

My long hair drifts around me like seaweed. The cold water pushes me to and fro and I sway with it, letting my arms undulate. Delicate white fingers of light stretch down towards me, making shadows dance on my pale skin.

All around, clicks and squeaks are the background music of my life and I barely hear them. Fish flicker past, silver and blue, their blank black eyes dismissing me. Much as my father always does.

I grind my teeth then force my shoulders to relax. He will see sense. He must. He will listen to my nephews, Bythos and Aphros, when they plead my case. He cannot make me marry one who, it is whispered, beats his concubines; brands them with steel hot from his forge.

But my father finds my very existence uncomfortable. Perhaps he will refuse to hear their plea. He has ignored me for the first sixteen years of my life, let my nephews raise me. I understand. In a way. I was born from an act of pure hatred. I remind him of his wife's anger and pain. So he pretends I am nothing.

Not all the love my nephews pour on me has ever quite made up for that. And all the stories they told me of the other gods—my family—just dug the chasm of loneliness deeper into my heart. How I wished to ride on Helios' chariot, to study medicine with Apollo, to play at war with Ares, to hunt with Artemis.

But I am alone. Outcast.

I want to blame someone. To hate someone in turn for what hatred did to me. Bythos and Aphros are impossible to dislike, though. And hating my father is pointless—he takes no notice of the world. Not since his wife, Gaia, convinced my Uncle Kronos to castrate him with a stone sickle. Not since Kronos flung Ouranos' manhood and the sickle into the sea. Not since my birth.

Hating Gaia and Kronos is pointless, too, for Kronos is imprisoned in Tartarus and Gaia's thoughts are fixed on events so distant I can barely comprehend them. I doubt she knows I exist.

And my mother, Thalassa, is the ocean. She who birthed me and sustained me. Her depths immeasurable. Her generosity uncountable. Her temperament unpredictable. Stormy, calm, deadly, bewitching in turns. How could one hate such endless blue-green beauty and fathomless blackness?

So the only thing left to hate is myself.

And I do. I hate the plump breasts and curved hips that have come to my body in recent years. Disdain the long hair that glistens like black glass. Loathe the eyes as dark as the ocean depths, lips of coral red, skin the colour of gold sand beaches.

Because every human and every god who looks upon me sees nothing else. They swoon over the eyes, the hair, the breasts. They write songs to the skin, the lips, the hips. They swear undying love when what they want is to fill with their lust what they see as an empty vessel.

I have a room full of their tainted treasures. They offer gold, silver, gems. They promise they can't live without me. But somehow they find a way after they see Bythos and Aphros' glares. After feeling the prick of cold bronze spears on heated skin.

Not once do they ask me what I want—or even *if* I want their gifts and their desire.

So far my nephews have managed to rid me of these silly boy-men; these would-be lovers who puff out their chests like full sails, then change direction, as fickle as the wind, when they hear a siren's song or spy a nymph's shapely legs. So, as long as I stay wrapped my mother's watery embrace, I have protectors. I am safe from the unfettered, festering lusts of men and gods.

But my nephews are restricted to my mother's realm by their fish tails, even though their horse bodies carry a man's chest and head. And I cannot stay here much longer. For my father has pledged me in marriage to a monster. Today he will come for me—unless my nephews can convince him otherwise.

So I wait, holding to the rocky sea bottom, to the lingering illusion of my safe childhood, listening to the clicks and groans of the ocean, the language of fish and lobsters, the bewitching longing of sirens on their isles. I close my eyes and let the gentle wash of waves overhead rock me like a babe.

A dolphin circles me, chittering a curious question and nudging me with her hard nose.

I push her gently away and shush her noisy squeaks. She has been sent by Aphros and I have no wish to hear his regret right now. I want to hope, just for a little longer, than he and Bythos have changed Ouranos' mind. That I will not marry that sweating, soot-stained, crippled oaf on the morrow. That I can stay in the clean, cool of the ocean forever.

A pair of misshapen shadows fall over me and I must open my eyes.

"Aunt . . . Daughter," By says. He has always found it strange that he is older, but I am the aunt. His wide-set eyes slide from mine and he presses his lips tight. His brow clouds and he removes his crown of coral and pearls, turning it in his hands.

Aphros speaks for him, as always, his smile light and hopeful, as always. "Aphrodite, your father would not change his mind." He lays a gentle hand on my head and strokes my hair as he did when I was small and frightened. "He insists. You must marry Hephaestus. But you are our brave girl. You will be alright."

The small pearl of hope I had carried in my breast dissolves, lodging as a lump in my throat. But I refuse to shed tears. What use would they be here, lost in the salt of my mother's perfection?

"Will I have to live . . . on land?" My words emerge broken and I swallow down the ache and lift my chin. I am Aphrodite, daughter of the sky and the ocean. I am strong and eternal, as they are. I am brave, as my nephews are.

Bythos nods, silent, his jaw working.

Aphros sighs. His wide mouth droops. "Yes. Hephaestus wishes you to reside with him in Mount Aetna. Help him tend the forge and fire. Help him make tools for the gods. He saw you once, as you walked on the sands of Cyprus. Saw you and loved you."

"But why him? Countless others have wanted me and always been refused. Why am I being given to a bitter, ugly cripple?" I cry. "As a slave to fan his forge and his body's fire? Sent to live in exile inside a mountain. Am I never to see the ocean again? To see you again?"

Aphros catches me against his chest, his cold tail coiling around me. "Ah, child, I'm sorry. Not given, sold. Your father, Ouranos, has bartered you for a spear of such power that he may prick holes in the night sky and create new stars."

I pull back, mouth agape. "Is that my worth? A spear for my virginity and this . . ." I sweep a hand down my curved body ". . . *shell* they all find so irresistible."

I stalk across the gritty ocean floor, tearing seaweed free and crushing it in my hand. I spin back and glare at my nephews. "What if I refuse? What if I stay here? My father can't very well come into Thalassa's domain."

My nephews glance at each other, their eyes wide. They speak silently, mind to mind, as only they can. Bythos frowns and nods. Aphros tilts his head, his expression anxious, his hands spread wide. Bythos presses his lips thin and glares.

Aphros' shoulders sag and I hide a smile. I have won. I know it. They will help me hide from my father and my husband-to-be. For Hephaestus cannot abide the water lest it quenches his fire. And Ouranos can only see himself endlessly reflected in my mother's serenity.

I return to my coral cave to sleep, content that I am safe awhile longer.

But in the darkest hour of night, a tempest tosses the sea, stirring sand into storms and waking me from dreams of fire and lust. A distant pounding of surf on land thrums through my chest. The crack of lightning and rumble of thunder is audible even so far below the sea's turbulent surface.

My sheltered rooms shake and grind. Pieces of coral and rock tumble, clouding the water and sending fish and crabs scuttling for cover.

Bythos and Aphros appear at my door. They are pale, their scales shimmering in the glimmering phosphor of the disturbed waters. Their hooves drum on rock, echoing thunder.

Aphros wrings his hands, flinching at the sound of Thalassa's fury and Ouranos' rage boiling overhead. "Your father and mother are at war over your refusal," he blurts. "Your mother sent us to rouse you. She cannot protect you any longer. We cannot stand against your father, either. I'm sorry." He holds out his hands, offering useless sympathy to ease his own grief. "I'm so sorry. You must be brave, child."

I ignore his touch and turn to Bythos. "Must I truly go?" I await his answer as the ocean's roar and rush surges around us. Bythos nods, not meeting my eyes. I wrap my arms around myself. If he sees no way of keeping me safe, then there is none for he has always been my fiercest protector.

I run my hands down my body. The body made from hatred and anger. Made for others to love and desire. It is no longer mine. Was it ever? What choice do I have?

Pain and loss clog the words in my throat and I turn to leave.

Aphros takes my hand, walking by my side. He pauses. "Bythos? Will you come?"

I glance back. Surely he won't abandon me now?

Bythos hesitates. "I will join you at the surface. There is a gift I wish to give our daughter. I will fetch it." He kisses my cheek and hurries away, his tail flickering in the uncertain light.

When I emerge from the sea I am clothed in a gown of water in shades of blue and green and deepest black. A string of silver-grey pearls adorns my neck. My mother's parting gift. A thin veil of silvery water sheets before my face and vanishes into steam at my feet, so I seem to walk on fog.

The instant I step onto the sandy Cyprus shoreline, the storm falls into eerie silence. Thick, tumbled clouds scud away, fading into wispy tendrils. The vast, black sky appears, speckled here and there by glittering diamond stars. I survey it critically. Father is right, the black canopy does need more stars.

But that doesn't change the fact that I am being traded for a weapon. A pointed stick.

Helios' chariot begins its daily trek across the sky, throwing cloth of pink and orange over the stars.

With my heart still sunk to the depths of the sea, I lift my face to Ouranos' domain and call to the gods.

"I am here, Father. I will wed Hephaestus with my feet in my mother's body, so my nephews can attend me. Come if you will."

When Ouranos and Hephaestus arrive, my father already carries his precious spear. Twice the length of a man and made of steel that shines purple-blue in the dawn light. My father caresses it with a lover's hand and plants the shaft in the golden sands, sending up sparks. He wears robes the colour of storm clouds and his feet are bare. His dark eyes gleam with satisfaction. I keep my face still and turn to greet my husband-to-be.

Hephaestus has adorned his hunched body with molten-steel-red robes. His thick-fingered hands are blackened with soot. His glittering eyes are small and close over a blade-nose. Eyes as black and opaque as the coal he burnt to forge the spear.

"You have no ladies to attend you?" His deep voice rumbles in a twisted barrel chest. "To bathe you?"

I gesture at the sea behind, where Aphros waits in the clear green shallows. "I need only my nephews. My mother's tears and my own bathed me." Will Bythos return? I feel unstable without his support.

"Let us begin!" My father spreads his arms wide and the beach fills with the pantheon.

I shrink back, my heart stuttering. I know none of them. I have lived isolated, hearing of the other gods only in bedtime stories from Aphros' indulgent lips. One by one they approach and greet me. Their names and faces are a blur: Hera, Zeus, Apollo, Hades, Artemis, Poseidon. All distant, aloof, bored almost. The women scornful, the men desirous, lustful.

Until one. Ares, tall and strong; seemingly sculpted of bronze and gold, with thoughtful eyes. He greets me with a warm smile and bows over my hand. The brush of his skin makes me gasp. His grip tightens and he kisses my cheek. The veil of water parts to let him close.

"Lift your chin, my sweet," he murmurs. "This will soon be over. Then the time will come for you to make a choice. Call on me when you are ready."

I swallow, my knees weak at the warm scent of his skin. I nod dumbly, not understanding. What choice can I possibly make? My destiny is written in the stars by my father. He and my husband-to-be own me. I care not. Cannot afford to care.

But I turn to my husband-to-be with my heart inexplicably lighter and my thighs trembling. Hephaestus takes my hand and I force myself not to recoil. His calloused fingers are gritty and leave streaks of black on mine. The pores on his face are black, too. His teeth broken. His hair matted with sweat and stinking of sulphur.

A glance at Ares stiffens my resolve. I am brave.

The ceremony lasts all day and into the evening. I stand numb and without words, watching others dance and drink and toast my beauty. Only Ares watches me with a sympathy in his eyes that almost breaks my heart.

The rituals end, at last, when Hephaestus parts the veil of water over my face. He smiles, his fingers stroking my cheek. When I pull away he grips my chin and tilts my face up.

"Oh, no, little fish. You're mine, now," he murmurs. "That body belongs to me."

The pantheon have gone, leaving only Ouranos on the beach. Darkness seeps across the land and into my heart.

Behind me, in the water, Aphros still waits alone. I hear his cries to my father. Hear him beg Ouranos to intervene as Hephaestus tears at my gown and prepares to take me there and then.

But my father has eyes only for his spear and simply smiles.

"Wait!" Bythos' cry gives Hephaestus pause. In the shallows, Bythos holds out his arms to me. "I have not yet given our gift to the bride. It is tradition."

Hephaestus releases me and I fall into Bythos' arms, sobbing.

He holds me away and gazes into my face. "Remember, daughter, you are the Goddess of Love and Beauty. You are strong and brave."

Beside him, Aphros nods and touches my hair. "And love is gentle, kind, and generous. Be good. Be submissive and he may treat you kindly."

I glance back at Hephaestus and shudder. But what can I do? He owns me, now. My body is his plaything.

Bythos shakes my shoulders, his dark eyes boring into me. "Love is also fierce, daughter. Fierce and protective. But you cannot love others unless you first love yourself. You cannot honour others unless you first honour yourself."

I frown, not understanding. Bythos takes my hand and presses something cold and hard into it. A curved stone weapon. I gasp. He nods. The sickle is only the length of my forearm. I turn it over, running a finger along the gleaming, scalloped obsidian edge. Blood beads on my fingertip.

I smile. "Thank you. I will go, now."

I stride back onto the beach and face my husband. Naked and defiant, I stand before him and hold the gleaming obsidian blade to his throat. He tries to push it aside, disdainful. But he has no power over the weapon. He controls metal and fire. I am water and stone.

"I may be your wife, but you will not touch me," I say, though my heart pounds and my mouth is dry. He is huge, his arms as thick as my thighs. He could break me in a moment. No! I grip the sickle tight and lift my chin. Aphros and Bythos have raised me to be brave. And Ares' sultry voice dances in my mind. He will have me first. None other. Not if I can help it.

Hephaestus' dark brows draw close together. His lips curl into a snarl. He stalks to my father's side and yanks the spear from Ouranos' grasp. The tip points toward my chest.

"Yield or I will destroy what you value most," Hephaestus growls.

I sneer. "If you mean this body, then so be it. You will not have it, either."

He hesitates, his eyes narrow. Then he hurls the spear. Past me. Into the water. I cry out and lunge for the shaft, but it slips through my fingers unchecked.

The spear passes through Aphros' throat and impales Bythos' chest. My nephews—my true fathers—they die without a cry. With their bottomless eyes fixed on mine, filled with love and regret. Their blood billows and swirls in the clear water, staining it scarlet.

I cover my mouth to stifle a scream. I feel the spear as though it skewered my body. Would that it had. I was a fool to think I could defy my husband and father. To think that my body was my own to give as I chose, when I chose. To think I had any value beyond that of a vessel for lust. My arrogance has cost the lives of the gentlest and kindest of my family.

"Come, daughter," Ouranos' brisk voice reaches me. "Go with your husband in peace. Look." He gestures and the spear slides free of the bodies and returns to his hand. I ache to hold Aphros and Bythos again. To have my loving fathers stroke my hair and tell me stories. But it is not to be. I have failed them. Failed myself.

Ouranos gestures again and the twin bodies dissolve into sparkling gems. With the spear he pierces the sky's velvet darkness. The glittering lights that were my fathers float high and nestle into the holes Ouranos made. Sixteen new stars. Two fish tied together forever in the heavens.

Tears gather and slip down my cheeks, forming a new gown of opaque silver over my body, hiding me from my husband's lewd gaze.

Bythos' words return to my thoughts. To love others, I must first love and honour myself. How can I be the Goddess of Love, otherwise?

I draw a deep breath and throw my shoulders back. I will not let them die in vain. I will honour myself. I will not be a plaything for anyone, god or man. I will choose my own lovers, my own path, my own destiny.

Staring into my husband's hot eyes, I speak clearly enough for all the world to hear. "You shall not have me, husband. Be content with your concubines and your forge. This . . ." I point to my body ". . . is mine, not yours. Come near and I will castrate you with the same knife that took Ouranos' manhood."

I hold up the sickle and it glints in the starlight.

About the Author:

Aiki Flinthart has 13 published novels and one non-fiction book, along with numerous short stories published in various anthologies and e-magazines. Her stories have been shortlisted in the Australian Aurealis Awards and she has been twice a top-8 finalist in the USA Writers of the Future competition. When not writing, Aiki likes to practice fantasy-approved hobbies such as martial arts, archery, knife-throwing, lute-playing, and belly-dancing. You can find her on Facebook, Twitter, and Instagram—she's the only Aiki Flinthart—and here:
www.aikiflinthart.com

ESCAPE

Tee Linden

trapped in the path of a whirlwind.
the sour fury of an ancient godeater approaches,
multi-mouthed and slithering.

flimsy skin splits along twin seams.
revealing plated scales made of star fire,
like shimmering chainmail.

slippery neon bodies
      escape
shooting up through cottonseed cumulus.
out to the protection of
      the cool cosmic dust.

celestial changelings tether themselves
with hot threads made from the stuff of shining giants
to swim the starlight seas of the infinite.

photophoric forms absorb the breath of the void.
shining tails flick rivers through the light years
making their way
      becoming again.

About the Author:

Tee Linden is a writer living south of Sydney. She loves writing SFF, especially if it involves the Australian bush. You can find her tweeting under @tearannosaurus or her website is teelinden.com

THE BETRAYAL OF IKHTHUS

Austin P. Sheehan

We were defeated. I knew it in my bones. Looking back, our mission had been doomed from the start. When our fleet left the bay of Timos, we had been beset by ill omens; portents of failure, portents of doom. Not that there were ever shortages of those in times of war.

The war between Thalassia and the treacherous Valakians had gone on for years, and the once fertile stretch of land that joined our two kingdoms was knee-deep with the dead. But during the dark and bitter winter, the Valakians had invaded the neutral island kingdom of Orten, attempting to intimidate them into an alliance. Royal messengers arrived—disguised as merchants—who called upon our leaders for aid. They outlined a clever strategy: thirty Thalassian ships and three of our precious magi—Wind, War and Sea—in a mission to free their kingdom, win their alliance, and thus tip the balance of war in our favour.

As winter loosened its hold upon the earth, our thirty ships had left the Thalassian bay on a mission to turn the tide of war against the Valakians. Three brave leaders lead our forces, each with ten ships of fighting men and a magi. Tesserarius Encanno's magi was the Servant of Tyndaridae, third of the ancients, ruler of the wind. Tessararius Homata was appointed the Servant of Toxotes, the ninth ancient, the God of war. Tessararius Nahuma was appointed the Servant of the twelfth ancient, Ikhthus, whose domain was the sea.

Before we had lost sight of our homeland, the fleet encountered ill omens, which foretold betrayal, fire, and an angry, bloodthirsty sea. Thinking to outwit the gods, the Tessararia Encanno, Homata and Nahuma decided to split the fleet for a three-pronged attack. Only the mages—elderly, wizened and bitter—urged caution, warning that the gods do not like to be tricked.

Two days after the fleets separated, the southerly skies turned dark and we were assailed by heavy gusts of wind. Trierarchus Massai, who had traversed these seas before, gave the order to furl the sails, hold our course and row. Strong winds were not uncommon at the end of winter, so Tesserarius Nahuma heeded his advice.

Huddled belowdecks, there was little for us soldiers to do but play dice or watch the rough sea and grey sky from the ship's sidescuttles, which let light and fresh sea air into the cramped quarters. Before long, soldiers—on the lookout for land, fish or sea siren—saw fog approaching, surrounding us. *Another ill sign.*

"These winds, the rough seas, and now fog." The deep voice of Kova, our keenly-forged Decanus, rumbled behind me. "I do not hold with this talk of omens, but how can we be certain of our bearings?" His query echoed my own, though I was in no position to voice it.

We were near the stairs the deck and were fortunate to hear Tesserarius Nahuma ask the same question.

"Trierarchus, what is this fog? How has it not been blown away by the mighty wind?"

"That's the Notia Omichlia, the fog of the southern ocean." Massai's voice was full of confidence. "These seas are full of mystery, Tesserarius Nahuma. But have no fear, we have not been blown off course."

"Thank the ancients, thanks to Tyndaridae," said Nahuma.

As Decanus Kova reassured the soldiers with Massai's words, mutterings of thanks to the ancient ruler of the winds echoed amongst the soldiers, and our concern eased.

For the next hour, despite the ship rolling against rough seas, we relaxed. We were confident in Massai's words, assured of the protection of the gods.

With a bone-jarring crunch, the ship jerked to the side, throwing us against the wall. Salt water sprayed through the sidescuttles, covering us all without regard to rank or honour.

"The fog has concealed a violent tempest!" Treirarchus Massai's shouted from above. "To the deck, soldiers!" roared the Decanus. "Perhaps our strength can assist in this battle against the sea!"

I fought down the fear in my stomach and followed Decanus Kova. As we reached the open sky, the heavens opened up and rain sheeted down on us. Howling winds tore at our sails and ferocious waves burst through the fog, towering over our ships.

"Decanus, go rouse Magi Algerbon," Tessarius Nahuma yelled. "Have him call upon Ihkthus to soothe the treacherous sea!"

As Kova returned below decks, we were hit by another wave. The force jerked soldiers off their feet and into the dark, churning depths. I slipped, crashing to the deck, the weight of my armour dragging me towards the edge. Tessarius Nahuma's hand reached for mine as I slid past, destined to the depths. I caught his hand, righted myself and grabbed the mast, shaking with fear.

"Grab ahold of something or go downstairs!" the Trierarchus shouted as we were hit by yet another wave. "My crew and I will try to turn us against the waves and the wind, but only experienced seafarers should hazard our aid."

"I will stay and help," Nahuma declared.

"Very well, but I suggest the rest of your soldiers go and pray with the Servant of Ikhthus!"

From belowdecks came the murmured incantation of Magi Algerbon. As the ship pitched and tilted, I did not loosen my grip on the mast. Below me, the voices of the soldiers repeated the chants of the mage, amplifying his pleas to the ancients to calm the seas. With my knuckles white against the mast, I did the same.

After several harrowing hours the tempest died away and the seas calmed. Our fleet had been reduced to six ships: two had snapped their masts when the powerful gusts had caught their poorly furled sails. Two more were lost to the waves. But we took solace; we had faced the worst of it and the other two fleets would have been unscathed by the storm that caused us such harm. We had no way of knowing how wrong we were.

The next day we sighted the coast of Orten; mountainous and rugged, green and full of life. A bay surrounded by dense trees and steep hills was where the Royal Messenger suggested a fleet land. It felt as if the gods had smiled upon us again. Tessarius Nahuma sent a scouting party into the mountains. As we awaited their return we unloaded our supplies.

It was the glow of fire in the hills above that was the first sign we had yet again been deceived, been betrayed.

The familiar shriek of a Valakian war trumpet split the silence of the secluded bay. In an instant, the sky was full of flaming arrows. Thin trails of smoke described their passage as they passed overhead and down towards the ships.

Tessarius Nahuma jumped into action, shouting orders above the chaos. "Soldiers, defensive positions! Archers, draw."

We rushed into our defensive formation, four ranks of one hundred soldiers, bristling with sword and spear, two rows of a hundred archers behind us.

There was no movement in the hills, just another volley of arrows.

Nahuma glanced at the ranks of soldiers, then up at the hills surrounding us. "Decanus Kova, take your soldiers into the mountains and engage those archers."

I swallowed, and following Kova's lead, rushed for the cover of the trees. We saw even less under the thick branches, which had kept their leaves despite the recent winter. The dense foliage muted the sounds of our comrades, all we could hear were our own footsteps, our own panicked breaths.

"What are the Valakians doing here?" I asked in a whisper.

"What happened to the arrangement the Ortens made?" Sophanus asked.

"Shh," Kova hissed. "The only way to find out is to get through this." He signalled for us to press on.

The hill was steep, and we had to sheath our weapons and use the trunks and branches of trees to pull us up. Every sense I had told me something was wrong. The Valakians should not have been there, should not have been ready for us.

A low rumble shook the ground, accompanied by the sound of tree trunks splitting. *Oh no.*

"What's that?" Sophanus asked as our eyes scanned the mountains above for the source of the noise.

"There!" A sphere of light—a ball of fire—was hurtling towards us. It crashed into trees, threw them out of its way.

"Return to the boats!" Decanus Kova yelled, recognising the threat.

We turned and ran down the mountain, straight into a row of advancing swords and shields.

"Tessarius, we must return to the boats!" Kova urged, panic rising in his voice.

"I say when we retreat!" Nahuma said, his voice firm.

"We have no—" Screams from the soldiers drowned out Decaus Kova's voice as three fireballs burst through the trees, cutting through rows of warriors, and continued on towards the ships.

"Soldiers of Thalassa, return to the boats!" Nahuma cried, too late.

Our ranks broke just in time to see a ship explode in flames. Treirarchus Massai and his men pushed a ship out of the way of the second fireball, and the third narrowly missed another ship.

"'Ware the archers!" roared the Decanus and Tessarius, to no avail. In a panic, we waded into the sea, so preoccupied with returning to the ships that many forgot to defend themselves from the arrows falling from the sky.

By the time another of our ships had been destroyed and the last of the men had boarded the remaining four ships, the beach was covered with corpses, the sea red with blood.

Tessarius Nahuma, Magi Algerbon, and the Trierarchi of the surviving ships debated long about the disaster that had befallen us, about we should do. Either the King of Orten had allied with the Valakians and had betrayed us, or the Valakians had overrun Orten during the winter, either learning of our arrangement or chancing upon us. They made the decision to travel north, find where Tesserarius Encanno had landed, and join our forces. Together we would get our revenge on the Valakian horde.

That night, those of us who could sleep dreamt either of bloody revenge, or of the ancients turning upon us and leading us to our ruin. No matter what our dreams, we woke to the sound of wood splintering, of our ships shuddering. My heart sank. We had run aground. The angry seas were not done with us yet. Only one of the ships had avoided the submerged reef, and it was not big enough to carry the surviving soldiers. Nahuma ordered the soldiers to shore, and many voices asked if we had angered the ancients, whether the Servant of Ikhthus had done enough to ask for the sea God's blessing.

Magi Algerbon's response was curt. "The Gods' plans can be hard to fathom. And Ikhthus, the ancient in all his power, does not control the shape of the land. Hidden reefs do not answer to him."

Nahuma urged haste. He had no doubt that the Valakian army was watching our fleet and would soon be on our heels. We began our trek through the low hills of Orten towards the city of Akagine, where we hoped to find sign of Encanno's army.

For over a week we pushed north. The Valakian horde pursued us, and we had to fight just to survive, barely escaping the clutches of the enemy time and time again, and we had still seen no trace of Tesserarius Encanno's army. Our mighty force, once numbering one thousand, had been reduced to just eighty, and none of us were without our scars.

As the sun set, casting an unearthly orange-red glow, hundreds of Valakian soldiers appeared from the low hills to the south. The silver of rectangular shields, the tips of countless spears and curved blades reflected the sickening orange glow. From the north came the sounds of hundreds of marching feet. Another army. My heart rose, surely this must be Encanno's force. But no, I looked north to see the pennons and bandums attached to their spears were the grey and blue of Orten.

As the two armies linked up and surrounded us, I knew it was over. We were defeated. We had been betrayed from the start. My tired, aching muscles wanted to give up, to lay down in the sand like so many of my comrades. Like them, I wanted to be carried by the ancient ones to the eternal battle grounds, to feast with the worthy. My time had not yet come, but it was close, so close.

The enemy soldiers shuffled aside and a wheeled platform was pushed forward. On the platform were three iron cages, two occupied by the emaciated figures of the Magi who had travelled with Tessarius Encanno and with Tessarius Homata;

the Servant of Tyndaridae and the Servant of Toxotes. Their hands were bound, their mouths gagged.

"Soldiers of Thalassa, Defensive formation!" Tesserarius Nahuma shouted. We formed two lines of thirty in front of our archers. Behind them stood Magi Algerbon, the proud and defiant Servant of Ikhthus, the twelfth of the ancients, the ruler of the sea.

"Your other armies have been beaten." A rough voice boomed from the Orten line. "You cannot hold any hope of victory!"

"Tesserarius Nahuma, you are surrounded. Surrender your magic-maker, your evil one, and we will show you mercy." The strong voice of the Valakian cornicern echoed above the crashing of the waves. "You have been betrayed. Your gods are dead."

Nahuma ignored the taunts from the enemy commander's herald, as he had before every battle. My eyes met his; haggard, grey and defiant. A hint of a smile on his dry, cracked lips. I prayed he would live to ignore the cornicern yet again.

"Magi Algerbon, our need is mighty. You must try again to call upon the ancient Ikhthus for aid!"

"I will do what I can, Tesserarius," the mage replied, his voice fraying against the wind. "But the lives and wishes of men matter little to the gods."

"Perhaps, yet they matter a lot to me. You must do this."

Algerbon—weak of flesh but unyielding in faith—began his murmuring of an invocation, filling the air with his potent chants, making my hairs stand on end. From the ranks of enemy soldiers came the slow rhythmic banging of war drums, trying to drown out his voice. He would not be cowed and his fraying voice rose, chanting in rhythm with the drums, accenting and strengthening his invocation.

A shrill trumpet blast filled the air. The Valakian forces pressed forward. Step by step they marched down to the beach, the sunset reflecting off their armour, and the leather-bound ranks of the Orten soldiers followed suit.

Snakes of fear burst to life in my stomach, constant companions over the last weeks of endless conflict. I clutched my shield, already dented and scarred from countless blows, and prayed to the ancients that it would protect me again.

Nahuma stepped forward, commanding our attention. He spat towards the line of overwhelming enemy soldiers. "We'll not be defeated by these bastards."

His calm defiance soothed the snakes in my stomach. He was not afraid. Perhaps there was still a way out of this. Perhaps he had faith that the ancient Ikhthus would sense our need, would respond. And if not, we would die as heroes and join the eternal feast.

"Archers ready!" Nahuma's voice was cold and firm. There was no one who could hear it and not obey.

My heart beat faster as the soldiers approached and I tightened my grip on the handle of my sword.

"Archers, release!" A volley of arrows shot overhead. As they hit their mark and enemy soldiers fell, inspired by Magi Algerbon's frantic chanting, the eager fire of battle coursed through my veins. I was ready to defend the Tesserarius, my comrades, and the Magi of Ikhthus to the death.

Before the archers could launch another volley, the approaching soldiers faltered, a peal of thunder sounding over the ocean.

A silver flash split the dark sky, heavy clouds full of rain, full of anger. The Valakian war drums were silenced, the only sound over the waves crashing was the Magi's fierce cry, "It is done!"

His words filled me with a dreadful, dark hope. As I turned to look, my heart sank. A mountain of water sped towards us.

"Soldiers of Thalassa, servants of the ancient twelve, pray to Ikhthus and you shall be spared!"

I bowed by head, welcoming death. Welcoming the arrival of the ancient and powerful Ikhthus.

My heart beat once, twice, and the wave was upon us, rushing through us with a bone crushing force, as if all the anger of the sea had been united into one unstoppable wall of death. I heard nothing but an ear-splitting roar and screams of terror.

The smell of the sea was stronger than I expected in the afterlife. I knelt on the damp ground in prayer, in gratitude. It was finally over. Familiar cries of pain and fear broke through the thunder. I opened my eyes, ready for a glimpse of the eternal battlegrounds.

My heart lurched. I was back on the endless Orten beach, the sea lapping at my wrists. Before me, Magi Algerbon knelt in the water, arms raised to the heavens. Surrounding us were countless enemy bodies, their faces contorted in expressions of terror.

Something dark stirred in the ocean's depths, and the familiar snakes of fear returned. The water parted and a grotesque, gigantic figure burst from the waves, towering over us. I wanted to turn, to run, but I was like a stone, unable to look away from the creature's massive head with a wicked elongated face and black eyes.

Icicles of fear raced down my back as the creature's body emerged from the depths. Muscular arms, as wide as the trunks of the oldest trees, ended in massive serrated crab claws. *What was this monstrosity?* Its body was at least twenty spans across, covered with hair like seaweed, thick and black.

"Sons and daughters of Thalassia," intoned Magi Algerbon, his deep voice breaking through my fear. "Behold Ancient

Ikhthus, Ruler of the Deep, Twelfth God of the Eternal Twelve." *No!* The monster was a mockery of the icons of the benevolent sea-centaur. This thing was grotesque and radiated a sick malice. It just couldn't be.

The creature's eyes bored into me. Its laugh, like the crashing of the waves, echoed through my soul.

"Ikhthus the Ancient, the Victorious, the Ruler of the Deep," my voice intoned, in chorus with the other surviving Thalassian soldiers. I tried to close my mouth, to stop the words that had come, unbidden, from my lips.

"We look upon you and know salvation." *No!* "We will follow you to the darkest core of creation. Until our last breath, we will be bound to you." *NO!*

The ancient God turned, its long finned tail flicking out behind. Cascading laughter echoed through my skull as it sunk back into the dark, angry sea.

As the night chased the last of the sun's rays from the sky, waves crashed against the empty beach. All remnant of friend and foe had been claimed, and any trace of the betrayal of Ikhthus had been washed away.

About the Author:

Austin P. Sheehan is a writer of speculative fiction, a lover of language, literature and '90s TV. Armed with a psychology degree, he went out into the world to further study humanity, and now prefers the company of his wife and greyhounds.

Austin grew up in Victoria's high country, and despite living in Melbourne for ten years, still feels at home amongst the mountains. You'll often find mountains in his stories, whether they are science fiction, fantasy, alternative history or horror. To discover what secrets are hidden in the mountains, go to www.austinpsheehan.com or find him on twitter @AustinPSheehan.

Austin's novella 'Submerged City' *was published in 2019. His short stories have been published in* 'Beginnings' *and* 'Journeys' *(Deadset Press) and* 'A Bond of Words' *(Scout Media), and his microfiction appears in* 'Curses & Cauldrons' *(Blood Song Books) and the* 'Worlds' 'Monsters' *and* 'Apocalypse' *anthologies by Black Hare Press.*

FLIGHT 102

DM Burdett

I saw it again today.

It. *Her.*

The piece of wreckage—a mangled wing which had promised salvation but now offered only to carry my corpse—rocked me in slumber, but I awoke to a soft melody and lifted my head, squinting into the burning sun.

Her black eyes sparkled above the surf, much closer than before. Joyous. Mocking.

I saw her for the first time days ago. I forget how many days; I don't know how many pass when I close my eyes.

But it must be a while since that first glimpse; I was lifting a bottle to my lips when I saw her luminescent tail, the splash of angelic fins, and then her body rose from the water, vibrant black hair sticking to her bare back in rivulets. She watched me as I watched her. And then she was gone. Like a mirage.

But the bottles of water I'd scavenged from the crash are long gone.

My body is a dry husk, I feel my life slipping away like sand through an hourglass. I don't know what's real anymore.

Last night I saw the white kangaroo again, surrounded by its red plash, glinting in the moonlight. Out here in the middle of the ocean. I laughed, my burnt and blistered lips bled, my sun-scorched skin cracked. The roo, and its blood-coloured bed; I know it holds some significance, but I no longer recall its meaning. I cried empty tears. I don't know why.

I sleep for a while.

When I wake, it's dark but for the moon. She croons in my ear, a soft lullaby that eases my pain.

I know it's time.

I can hardly turn my head, but when I do, she smiles with teeth that shine in the sparse light. Teeth so sharp.

But her eyes, those deep ebony pools, wash away my thoughts. I smile as I drown in them. I smile as she takes her first bite.

About the Author:

DM Burdett was born in the UK, roamed as an army brat, and now lives in Australia where she spends her days avoiding drop bears and killer spiders.

She has published a Sci-Fi series, had some success with short stories and is currently working on a YA dystopian series.

She has worked in software development for three decades and has published two children's series on the subject.

A life of roaming the shores of Australia in her teardrop caravan calls to her but, until then, there always seems to be just one more software project to complete.
www.dmburdett.com

Mother of the Deep

Lisandra Linde

She didn't know if the parents had thrown the child overboard or if it had merely fallen, slipping from its mother's arms during the storm. Azurnai watched the little one streak through the dark water, its body white like a scallop's shell, the tuft of hair on its crown black as the inky depths Azurnai called home. She swam towards it, catching it on its way down. Its tiny form fit perfectly in the crook of her elbow, its head lolling back over the curve of her arm, dark hair brushing her cold, scaled skin. She'd seen many dead men drifting down to the sea bottom, falling like debris from the shattered hulls of the ships her children fed on. Their bodies thrashing enough to unsettle the bones from their sockets, then going limp as seaweed, fluttering down into the crevices of the seabed where the serpents waited open-mouthed and ravenous.

But those were men and, though the child had the same telltale appendage between its legs, it was far younger than the sailors and travellers who crossed the waves in droves. It was too young to make such a journey. Too young to be parted from its mother's breast. Azurnai stroked the child's face, a clawed finger tracing the open lips, the closed eyelids and small, silken lashes. The child was dead, but it looked peaceful. The dead often did. There was no point in making a fuss when one was dead, and the sleepy expressions of the corpses that plunged into the ocean's depths were almost always serene with acceptance, the muscles pried of any resistance they might have had in those final gulping, thrashing moments.

Had this child put up any resistance? She had not seen it until it delved down into the deep, towards the lightless realm where she held court. By then it was already limp, white as a fish's carcass. Azurnai had raised many children, some serpentine, others with fins and spines and bodies as large as ships. But she had never taken a human as one of her own. Humans did not belong in the depths, save as sustenance. Her children crushed and devoured their ships, yet more ships always took their place. Humans were not content to stay in their realm. They paid the price for their endless trespassing. But the child could not have chosen to cross the sea. The child had not been old enough to willingly place their life on the line to make the crossing. His innocence tugged at something deep within her.

She'd lain with a human once. A sailor who had taken her fancy. She could not say why. In fact, so many centuries had passed that she could not remember his face, nor what had drawn her to him. All she remembered was finding him clinging to the broken end of a ship's mast, watching her in awe and horror as she slipped from the water and onto one of the sharp rocks that had stranded him there. Long after his lifeless body had sunk to the ocean floor, a child had quickened in her womb. Their son had been half mortal, and born able to live as happily on land as underwater. But the human blood in him made him love the mortal world more than the sea and he had left her, and all his brothers and sisters, to live on land. Ever since then, she had avoided humans, leaving her children to feast as they pleased but never partaking herself.

She had named her son Amsentir, and his hair had been black as well. He had the brown skin of the Sestese, the people most determined to brave the waves to escape the tiny cluster of islands they called home. He had little of her in him, save her eyes—black and gleaming, able to see in the most lightless of places—and the breathless immortality that made her mistress of the seas. This tiny mortal nestled in the crook of her fin-tipped arm looked nothing like her. So mortal, so pale, so utterly lifeless.

Death's hold meant little to Azurnai. It was a process easy enough to undo. Some of her children had tasted harpoons and gunpowder, great metal balls ripping through their bodies, leaving them floating in pieces on the waves. Azurnai did not like to lose her children. She did not care what laws governed life and death on dry land. The gods and goddesses there may do as they please, but she would decide who lived and died in her sea. She patched her children with shell needles and jellyfish tentacles and breathed life back into their bloated bodies. They were never quite the same, but they were alive—in a fashion.

She stroked the infant's chubby cheek with a long, black talon. She had not taken a new child in a long time.

She had frightened mortals with her children, yet still they came in droves. Perhaps if they saw something more frightening than sharp teeth and scaly hides, they'd know better than to venture forth again. She held the infant up, watching its head roll back and bob on the ocean current, dark hair drifting like seaweed.

What could be more frightening than one of their own, but twisted into the stuff of darkness and nightmares? Azurnai smiled to herself, drawing a talon along the side of the infant's neck, pulling open the virgin skin, peeling it back with line upon line. A creature of the sea needed gills, after all. Red danced in the water like smoke, rising up from the child, a final flag waved for mortality. Azurnai dug her fingers into the tiny chest, slicing her way through sinew and bone until she felt the warmth of the infant's heart sitting in her palm. Deathless things had no need of hearts, but she had need of loyalty. She should have taken Amsentir's heart. She would not make that mistake again.

She plucked the heart out and pushed it past her blue lips, swallowing it down, feeling the warmth of the babe's last life-blood snaking down her throat. Then, with a tender squeeze, she brought the child to life in her arms. The infant opened its mouth to squall, bubbles fizzing from its newly carved gills.

"There, there, my little one," Azurnai purred, a hand placed over the child's still-open chest. "No need to cry. Let me take you home to meet your brothers and sisters."

She slipped into the depths and watched as the infant opened its eyes, seeing for the first time through the darkness that blinded men. She felt a tremor in some hidden crevice within herself as the child squealed not in horror, but in delight at the waiting teeth and glowing eyes of his new family, waiting in the depths.

About the Author:

Lisandra Linde is a Norwegian-Australian writer and editor. She is a PhD student at Flinders University in Adelaide. When she isn't researching Australia's forgotten female essayists she writes fantasy and creative nonfiction. She might also be a witch—just ask her co-workers why she goes missing whenever there's a full moon.

Her work has appeared in 'Feminartsy', 'Tulpa Magazine' and in Bowen Street Press anthologies 'Pulse' (2017) and 'Tattoo' (2018). You can follow her on Twitter: @KrestianLullaby

SEABORN

Maddie Jensen

Jelly always said there was nothing like seeing Jupiter and the Galileans for the first time, and Andie had to acknowledge that her sister had been right. No amount of photos could have prepared her for this experience. Her fingers were pressed against one of the square windows on the side of the space shuttle, the thick glass cold beneath her touch.

"Looks like we got ourselves a newbie." Matthias Ryker, a biologist who'd made the six-month trip out from Earth alongside Andie, grinned at her awe.

"Shut up, Matthias." Andie drew away from the window to nudge him in the side. This was Matthias' second expedition out to the Galileans—he'd formerly been stationed on Callisto before a workplace incident had sent him home to Earth. Three years later and he was ready to make the crossing again, this time on the same project as Andie—the Ganymede terraforming expedition.

"Come on." Matthias beckoned her away from the window and toward the seats in the middle of the shuttle. "We're going to be landing in a minute, and it's usually pretty rough."

The pair had formed a fast friendship in the months of the crossing, and both of them had expressed excitement about their upcoming jobs on Ganymede. Matthias was also the only person that Andie had told about her sister's sudden disappearance. That was the real reason she had come out to Ganymede—the geologist job for the terraforming expedition had got her the ticket, but Jelly was the reason she'd wanted to head to the Galileans in the first place.

Jelly had been missing for three months when Andie set out from Earth. In total, she'd been missing for almost a year now. Andie held out hope that someone would contact her on the crossing and let her know that Jelly had been found, that there had been some kind of mistake. Yet as time dragged on, Andie knew the chances of Jelly being found alive were slim to none.

Matthias had been supportive, but realistic. He hadn't wanted to give Andie false hope. Although he agreed it was odd that the officials on the expedition hadn't told her what was going on, Jelly being labelled MIA meant her crew probably didn't know what had happened to her.

The pilot announced that they would be landing shortly. Andie buckled up as they made their final descent toward Ganymede. They whizzed past Io and Europa, barely giving her time to take in the smaller moons. Callisto, the largest of the Galileans, loomed in the distance past Ganymede.

The most impressive of all was Jupiter itself, dwarfing the Galileans. When Andie craned her neck to look out again, she could see the Great Red Spot on the huge gas giant's surface. She remembered Jelly telling her that it was bigger than Earth. It had been one of the many random space facts she'd read out of a book to Andie when they'd been kids. Jelly had always loved space, had always wanted to explore the solar system and beyond. Before this trip, Andie had never been as brave as her sister.

The shuttle touched down with a bump, and Andie unwrapped her fingers from around the armrests of her seat. She hadn't even realised how tightly she was clutching at them until her body relaxed. Matthias slid out of his seat, bouncing on the balls of his feet with enthusiasm. He'd lamented just how much he'd missed the Galileans during his resting time on Earth, and he was eager to get back to work.

They stepped off the shuttle and into a large transparent dome. At a guess, it was an atmospheric dome that would protect them from the extremely thin amount of oxygen that made up Ganymede's air. She followed Matthias, her palms clammy. She wiped them on her pants, attempting to shake off the feeling that she didn't belong here.

"Matthias Ryker." A tall, lean man in his late thirties approached them. He had a friendly face and an easy smile. He held out his hand. "I'm Tomas De Souza, head of security here. I recognised you from the files transferred from Callisto."

"Good to meet you." Matthias shook Tomas' hand, before Tomas turned his attention upon Andie. Without comment, she presented her identification and staff file, which he examined intently.

"Andromeda James." He raised his eyebrows. "Any relative of Evanjelin James?"

"Yes." Andie's voice was cool. "She was—*is*—my older sister."

Tomas examined her calmly. She wondered if he was trying to see the similarities to Jelly. Andie was tall and dark-haired; Jelly was petite and blonde. They had the same hazel eyes, but not many people picked them as sisters.

"You're a geologist." Tomas' eyes flicked back to her staff file.

"Yep." Andie forced a smile. She wished she could appear eager about this adventure, but in truth she was impatient for answers on Jelly. "Do you know who I have to report to?"

"That would be . . ." Tomas checked over the file. "Dr Lerner, Head of Research."

"Perfect, thanks." Andie grabbed her bags and accepted a copy of the site map from one of the officials handing them out. She figured that she would go and get settled into her room and then introduce herself to Dr Lerner. It had been a long six months, but it would all be worth it if it meant obtaining answers.

Andie's room was small, as she had assumed it would be. At least it was private, unlike the bunks she had shared over the past few months during the crossing. Having her own space elicited a sigh of relief as she dropped her bags, collapsing on the narrow bed and ignoring how it creaked under her weight. She couldn't even find the energy to unpack, too concerned with taking stock of her new surroundings.

Andie didn't get much sleep the first night. Although the bed was certainly more comfortable than anything she'd slept on during the crossing, the knowledge that she was closer than ever to solving the mystery of Jelly's disappearance kept her awake. Every now and then, she peered out the window, wondering what lay beyond the dome. Someday soon, she expected that she would find out. As lights danced across the ceiling through the slits in the blinds, Andie drifted off to sleep.

When she woke up early the next morning and emerged from her room, Ganymede was busy. Andie's task was to map out future terraforming sites and deduce their viability, which would involve a lot of aerial research. Checking the map that had been given to her, she made her way to Dr Lerner's office.

The research centre smelled like a hospital room—chemical and sterile, like someone had just finished using cleaning products. Andie preferred the slightly musty smell of her room. Dr Lerner was a man in his sixties with a weathered face who offered Andie a warm smile as she made her way in.

"Miss James, welcome."

"It's a pleasure to meet you, Dr Lerner." His skin was dry and papery as she shook his hand. "I'm ready to head out wherever you need me."

Andie didn't know her exact role. She had applied for a geologist position and been accepted a few weeks later. The job ad had mentioned assessing the surface for viable life. She assumed she would be doing some mapping out of the terrain, ascertaining how much of the planet's surface was viable for terraforming.

"Oh, you won't be going beyond the dome. We need you here—in truth, we actually need you to assist in some of the work that your sister Evanjelin was doing."

It was the second time that Andie had heard her sister's name mentioned, and with just the amount of casualness as the first time. How could everyone be so blasé?

"What do you mean?" Andie shook her head vehemently. "I'm not a biologist, I'm a geologist. I don't think I can help you."

She wanted to ask what Dr Lerner knew about Jelly, but felt she was still too fresh to this place to demand answers on her sister's disappearance.

"It's not really a matter of either." Dr Lerner gestured for Andie to follow him. She didn't understand exactly what Dr Lerner was talking about—until they stepped into the next room. This one didn't smell like chemicals. Instead the air smelled like a fresh bout of rain—earthy and fresh.

Andie froze, taking in the huge glass tank in the centre of the room. There was something inside it—a fish-like, pale green creature that certainly wasn't like anything she'd seen back on Earth. Andie inspected the creature inside the glass tank with a mixture of horror and wonder. In some ways it looked humanoid, but in others it was certainly an alien. Its three-digit toes and fingers were webbed, and there were gills protruding from the sides of its neck. The creature stared at Andie with pitch-black eyes.

"What is this?" Her voice came out a reverent whisper, although she thought she already knew the answer.

"We call them the Seaborn." Dr Lerner came to stand beside her, folding his arms. There was a smugly satisfied smile on his face. "They're native to Ganymede."

Andie took a few more silent moments to examine the creature—the Seaborn. This was the first she'd heard about extra-terrestrial life on the Galileans, which meant this was relatively new and secret information. She pressed her fingers tentatively to the glass. The Seaborn blinked slowly, but had no other reaction.

"They're amphibious," Dr Lerner explained, "that means that . . ."

"I know what amphibious means," Andie responded, a little more sharply than she'd intended. She removed her hand from the glass, feeling the coolness leave her fingertips. The tank was large, but it seemed small for a creature the size of an average human being. She wondered if the Seaborn felt trapped.

"We've called her Storm," Dr Lerner looked at the creature, and then turned his gaze on Andie. There was something expectant in his eyes.

"Why do you need my help on this?" Andie demanded, feeling a bit betrayed. Whilst she'd come here with ulterior motives, she'd never suspected the terraforming expedition might have a different use for her as well. "What can I possibly do that Jelly couldn't?"

"Your sister was . . ." Dr Lerner looked down at his clasped hands. "She was on the brink of discovering a way to communicate with the Seaborn. Unfortunately, upon an excursion out to study them in the wild, she was killed by some of them. We were hoping that you might continue her work."

Andie fell into a shocked silence. She stared at the creature in the tank. Storm didn't look particularly dangerous, but the Seaborn were clearly more deadly than they appeared. She blinked away the sudden tears that welled in her eyes. She hadn't expected an answer so early on. She thought she'd have had to work for it. Yet Dr Lerner had put the truth about Jelly on the table from the very beginning. Andie had held out a sliver of hope that Jelly might be alive, but Dr Lerner's confirmation made a heaviness settle in the pit of her stomach.

"Oh." Was the only thing she could say, the only word she could manage. When she looked back to Storm, the Seaborn's gaze was fixed on Andie. She raised a webbed hand to point at something. Upset and unable to understand what the creature wanted, Andie murmured an excuse before leaving the room.

She knew Dr Lerner must think her terribly unprofessional, but she couldn't keep her composure now that she had learned how her sister had died. She secluded herself in her room for the rest of the day, unable to face the terrible truth of Jelly's fate.

It was late when Andie returned, her keycard for the facility giving her access to the room where Storm was housed. She wanted to examine the Seaborn away from prying eyes. Although Storm hadn't been the one that had killed Jelly, the creature might have answers as to why. Jelly had been close to discovering how to communicate with them. Andie wondered if she might be able to find out how.

She thought the creature might be asleep, but Storm watched her with those disconcerting black eyes. Andie swallowed hard, compelled to meet her gaze. She couldn't hate the Seaborn. Ganymede had been their moon, before the terraforming expedition took it from them. She was angry that Jelly had been killed by them, yet she wouldn't take her mixed emotions out on Storm. This creature was a prisoner, being studied and prodded at by people who sought to understand her.

Storm pointed again, raising her webbed fingers in the water. Andie followed the direction of her finger. She'd done this the first time that Andie had entered, and whilst she couldn't properly communicate with the Seaborn, it was obvious that there was something Storm was trying to tell her. She indicated one of the flat-screen computers, attempting to understand what Storm was pointing at.

"This?"

Storm shook her head.

Andie continued to point to items in the vicinity, amazed that Storm was able to comprehend, to an extent, what she was saying. She caught something tucked neatly onto one of the shelves above the computers. It was a notebook, and Andie's stomach lurched as she opened it to her sister's small cursive writing. These were Jelly's notes on the Seaborn.

"This?" she asked, her voice little more than a whisper.

Storm nodded.

Andie began to flick through Jelly's notes. The familiar handwriting made her ache with longing, despite knowing her sister was dead. Jelly had been attempting to communicate with the Seaborn using sign language and hand movements, due to their limited vocal capacity stemming from their amphibious nature. It explained why Storm had used her hands to point, relying on Andie's responses. Jelly had taught the captive Seaborn to nod for 'yes' and shake for 'no'.

When she looked up from the notebook, Storm was pointing insistently once again. After another series of trial and error, Andie realised that the Seaborn was miming writing motions with her webbed fingers. Andie searched around the room before handing Storm a waterproof marker.

Slowly but surely, the creature wrote down a series of numbers. They would have been backwards to Storm because to Andie they made perfect sense. A date from last year. A time stamp. She didn't understand what any of it meant, but she grabbed a pen and scrawled it underneath Jelly's last entry. Storm quickly used her hands to wipe away the numbers.

"Thank you," Andie said, although she wasn't entirely certain what she was thanking the Seaborn for.

Storm clasped her hands together in what any human would recognise as a gun motion. Unsettled, Andie took a stumbling step back and fled the room. With shaking fingers, she gripped the pen and wrote another note under the numbers that Storm had given her, a single word that made her feel nauseous.

Gun?

Discerning what Storm was trying to tell her was like solving a riddle. During the day, Andie would do her job—documenting any attempts made to communicate with Storm, for the most part. She utilised Jelly's notebook, but didn't allow any of the others to see the secret messages she'd gained from Storm. She also noticed that she was the only one Storm would 'speak' to; the Seaborn was stubbornly insistent on ignoring the others. Dr Lerner was delighted by this, but other biologists including Matthias openly expressed their frustration.

"I don't understand," Matthias admitted, "You're a geologist. Why is it that you're having the most success?"

Andie merely shrugged. She didn't know why the Seaborn trusted her. Perhaps it was that Storm saw Jelly in the shape and colour of Andie's eyes.

"The Seaborn don't distinguish me by my job title. Maybe Storm just thinks I'm trustworthy."

The fate of the imprisoned Seaborn wasn't a big deal to Andie. She didn't really know what was happening to the Seaborn in the wild, but she assumed they were being relocated to make way for the terraforming. She hadn't seen Storm openly experimented on. Andie was more determined to gain answers about Jelly, and it seemed as though Storm actually wanted to communicate with her. The real question was, what was Storm trying to say?

It struck her late one night when she was watching old videos of her and Jelly as kids. Each video had a date and time stamps throughout. Andie had originally thought perhaps the points were coordinates, but now she was forced to reconsider.

When she paused at one particular point, she realised that Storm had given her the date and time of a specific video. If Andie's calculations were correct, the video would have been right before Jelly had died.

Scrambling out of bed, Andie tiptoed into Storm's holding facility in her pyjamas. Throwing down Jelly's notebook, she pointed at the screens above the computers. Footage was taken of various places around the Ganymede terraforming expedition and displayed at all times. Storm pressed her fingers to the glass and nodded.

Andie sat down and logged into the main computer. Every staff member had access. Considering its funding, the terraforming expedition couldn't have anything to hide. They had to be transparent. However, Andie was the only one who knew where to look. She clicked into the surveillance footage data bank. With trembling fingers, Andie entered the date into the system, and then the time stamp.

Searching through the camera feeds, she finally found a video that had her sister in it. Although terrified at what she was about to witness, she paused only a moment before she clicked 'play' on the footage.

Jelly was standing between several Seaborn and a half-dozen armed Ganymede security members, her arms raised as if trying to nullify a tense situation. The dome and large terraforming machines could be seen in the background, so this must be some way out into Ganymede. The Seaborn were clutching what appeared to be glowing blue balls, some kind of technology that Andie didn't recognise. Were these weapons?

Andie turned up the volume so that she could hear what was being said. The audio feed must have been coming from microphones, since Jelly and the security team were all wearing atmospheric suits.

"They won't let any of the geologists or the terraforming team near them!" It was Tomas' familiar voice, indignant. "I understand you want to protect them, Evanjelin, but they're a nuisance to all of us."

"Didn't you stop to think we're the nuisance?" Jelly asked. She sounded so strong and assured. "We are the ones who landed on *their* moon. They're upset because we're changing the environment to one that suits us without even a second's consideration for them."

"They're amphibious." Tomas was growing more impatient. "They can survive in the water or something. Get out of the way so we can deal with this. These creatures killed three of the terraforming team."

"Oh, and the terraforming team did nothing?" Jelly's voice dripped with sarcasm. "These *creatures* are defending themselves, Tomas."

Tomas was quiet for a moment, but when he spoke again, his voice was low.

"I'm not going to ask again."

The Seaborn may not have known what was being said, yet they could sense the tension. One moved forward suddenly, and one of the security team opened fire. Jelly flinched, and a Seaborn hissed angrily and advanced on the team as another of the Seaborn collapsed to the ground.

One of the Seaborn hurled a blue ball at a member of the security team. He went down screaming, clawing frantically at his suit as his entire body pulsed with what appeared to be some kind of electrical bolts. When he fell, he didn't move again. The security team stood their ground, guns pointed at the Seaborn.

"No!" Jelly's voice was panicked. "Stop it! They didn't do anything wrong!"

She tried to put herself in between the two warring factions again, except things had already descended into chaos. A bullet pierced Jelly's bubble-like helmet and she collapsed onto the ground. Blood pooled out from her head. The bullet hadn't just shattered her helmet, it had gone straight into her forehead.

The motion Storm had made with her hands. The word Andie had scrawled into the notebook.

Gun?

Andie pressed her trembling hands over her mouth, tears streaming down her cheeks. Her sister hadn't been killed by savage Seaborn at all, but Ganymede terraforming expedition members wanting an excuse to continue their mission.

Tomas dropped his gun onto the ground, his hands shaking. He must have been the one who'd shot Jelly. He fell to his knees and pressed his hands over his head. The Seaborn were dead as well. The poor creatures hadn't stood a chance against bullets. One of the expedition team carefully gathered up the Seaborn's blue balls into a bag. Most likely they'd be taken in for examination, so the terraforming expedition could work out how to use the natives' own weapons.

"What the fuck do we do?" A team member asked, evidently panicking as he examined the ground littered with Seaborn bodies.

"We report this to the authorities," Tomas said, his voice hoarse. "We need to figure out a way to clean this up, and they'll know best."

Andie stopped the video, her heart thumping in her chest. Why hadn't they deleted the footage if they were covering up her death? Was it because they thought it would look too suspicious if there was a gap and no explanation? Storm had obviously seen the footage on repeat if she could remember the date and time stamp.

Andie wasn't upset anymore, she was angry. Her sister's death had been covered up, made to seem like a terrible accident. If it came out that the security team had killed her in the pandemonium, it wouldn't look good for the expedition. Blaming it on the Seaborn had killed two birds with one stone—a reason for Jelly's disappearance, and a way to keep their project going by blaming the natives.

"Andromeda?" It was Tomas, his voice making her jump. He approached her from the darkness with caution. "What are you doing here so late? I heard noises while on patrol and thought I'd check in."

Shoving herself away from the desk, Andie marched over to the confused head of security. His hand slowly went for his gun, but Andie was quicker, batting his hand aside and wrenching his gun from its holster. Tomas scrambled to take it back, but Andie had stepped away with the gun pointed at him. His dark eyes widened, expression confused.

"What the fuck?"

"I know what happened." Andie levelled the gun at Tomas' head. It shook in her hands as she blinked away tears. "I know you shot her when things got out of control."

Tomas' eyes flicked to the paused image of him on the ground, almost a year ago, trying to figure out how to make the murder he'd committed just go away.

Fuck this project, Andie thought venomously. *Fuck the natives dying just so humanity can get their greedy hands on another habitat they won't care for.*

"I didn't mean to," Tomas insisted, eyes wide and hands held high in surrender. "Andie, you have to understand, it was an accident."

"Maybe," Andie murmured, lowering the gun. "Your life isn't mine to take anyway."

She fired three shots into Storm's tank, fracturing the glass. It broke under the pressure of the water and Storm came tumbling out. Gun still in one hand, Andie held out her other hand to help the Seaborn to her feet. On her legs, Storm was half a head smaller than Andie. She examined her with those inquisitive dark eyes and Andie smiled.

"You can't do that," Tomas protested. "We need her to . . ."

"No." Andie spun him around and pressed the gun into the small of his back. "You're taking us to the armoury, now. Try anything stupid and I swear to God I'll put a bullet in you. I really want to, so don't tempt me."

Tomas kept his hands held up the whole way, and led her down the silent corridors of the facility until they reached the armoury. He withdrew his keycard and scanned it without a word. Andie was perturbed by his silence and compliance. He was the head of security, surely he was trying to figure how to get himself out of this mess. Storm accompanied them, webbed feet slapping unsteadily on the floor.

"What exactly is your plan?" Tomas demanded as Andie shoved him none too gently forward. She scanned the armoury, sizing up what weapons the security team had access to. Storm stayed in the doorway, shrinking away from the sight of all the guns and grenades. Andie couldn't say that she blamed her.

"While I'd love to burn this place down, it's not up to me to get revenge." Andie handed the grenade belt to Storm. The Seaborn accepted it, examining it quietly before nodding.

Tomas sneered. "You're giving weapons to the savages?"

"They're not savages," Andie snapped, whirling around to face him. She felt stupid for taking her eyes off him for even a moment. "They're natives. They're the Seaborn. We're the invaders."

"You sound just like Evanjelin." Tomas scoffed, and Andie punched him in the face. She wasn't an aggressive woman, but she would not hear Jelly's murderer speak her name. Her blood was pumping as Tomas staggered back, examining his bloody nose. Storm shrank away, clutching the grenade belt to her.

"Don't ever say her name."

"Bitch," Tomas snarled, and he backhanded Andie across the face so hard that he knocked her to the ground. Her head spun and her cheek throbbed, and Tomas grabbed her hair before she could scramble to her feet. "Do you really think I'm going to let you arm them?"

Andie lashed out at him again, but Tomas grabbed her wrists and pinned them above her head. He crouched over her, his free hand tightening around her neck. Andie tried to kick at him, but Tomas pressed his knee into her stomach. She should have seen something like this coming. She knew Tomas wouldn't take defeat lightly, but she'd underestimated him.

"What a shame." His dark eyes glittered with fury and triumph. "Both you and Evanjelin, tragically killed by the Seaborn."

Tomas' fingers tightened around her throat. Andie's vision swam and she choked for air. She was going to die here, another James sister whose murder Tomas would frame on the Seaborn. Then Tomas went flying and the pressure around Andie's neck released. She gasped for breath and rubbed at her throat, sitting up to see Tomas on the ground with a bloodied head. Storm stood over him with the belt of grenades Andie had given her.

Tomas' face contorted in rage and he lunged, but Storm hit him over the head again. He collapsed on the ground, and this time, the Seaborn didn't stop hitting him until he'd gone still. Blood poured from his head wound. Andie wasn't a medic, so she couldn't tell if he'd ever get up again. Taking a deep breath, she climbed to her feet.

"Come on. We need to move fast."

Storm followed Andie like a shadow as she departed and locked the armoury. Andie led the Seaborn to one of the series of double doors that led outside the airlock. She pushed the button to open the first door, and gestured for Storm to step inside.

"Thank you." She didn't know what else to say to her unlikely ally. If not for the Seaborn, Andie would probably still believe the lie about her sister's death. She might even be dead herself.

"Thank . . . you." Storm repeated the words. Andie didn't know if she was testing them out, or if she understood them and was issuing the sentiment back to her. Nonetheless, Storm's mangled attempt at English made her smile. Storm stepped outside as Andie closed the first door of the airlock and opened the second. The Seaborn headed away from the dome with a slow certainty, the belt of grenades clutched tightly in her pale green hands.

Once Storm was out of sight, Andie retrieved her case from her room and headed for the transit bay. Shuttles were constantly flying in and out, usually from the other Galileans but sometimes to the space station orbiting Jupiter. That was where she would catch an Earthbound ship. All she could do was hope that the Seaborn managed to do some damage of their own. Otherwise, she never wanted to think about the place where her sister had been killed and her death covered up to further the dreams of the megacorporations.

The pilot didn't appear impressed by a dishevelled young woman in pyjamas lugging a huge case onto the shuttle. She offered him a wide, toothy grin.

"It's not even five am local time." The pilot frowned. "Where are you headed?"

"I've been fired," Andie admitted, although she'd really just left the job of her own accord. "So you understand I'm pretty eager to get to the space station and make the crossing."

She wasn't the only passenger on board—a middle-aged woman arched her eyebrows and pursed her lips at Andie's appearance. She resisted the urge to flip her off and sank into a seat, pulling her case close. Exhaustion and satisfaction settled over her like a heavy blanket, and she leaned her head against the back of the seat and closed her eyes.

By the time the first explosion rocked Ganymede, Andie was already far away from the Galileans, and she never once looked back.

About the Author:

Maddie Jensen is a fantasy & science fiction author from Sydney, Australia. She has been reading and writing from a very young age, and is particularly invested in complex characters and well-written female protagonists.

TRIBUTARY

Rem Wigmore

In the mornings back before Latzamu burned, Enta Serzan would rise with the calling of the birds, Arca's breath barely warming rose into the sky. Serzan offered appropriate sacrifice to the river: the first fish they caught. The snared bird. The second-caught fish was always released back into the water, to show that people of Arcatan—and especially priests—knew to be proper custodians. No priest would never overfish the Huksha.

These mornings, Serzan can cast the line a full twelve times and draw no fish. In the last flooding, ash came up with the waters, not rich good silt.

How to be priest of a dying river?

The first answer is to pray. Arca guards the city and the land, Arca of the sun and pure fire. But Arca can't burn away invaders without burning all else, and bringing too soon the scourge of the world. Seven times seven times seven years it will be before the burning comes. In Serzan's worst moments, they hope to wake to the burning day. For their bitter grief to be turned pure into coals.

Serzan wishes most for the invaders and Latzamu the city by the river and all of it to be washed away, but the day does not come. So at last they wake with the calling of the birds and leave their ventarid and travel, running with the river, to the sea.

Half a league down the river from home, Enta Xyrma intersects them, keen and quick. He must have run to his boat when he saw them leave from his temple. He is serene and shows no signs of haste.

"Enta Serzan," Xyrma greets, their proper title. He smiles, as he always smiles. Though he wears his hair oiled into ringlets in the usual Chorage style, he lacks the beard Serzan has seen on every other priest of his type, only a merest peach fuzz over his soft chin. He has a face they want to trust.

"Enta Xyrma," they say deliberately. Xyrma nearly hides his wince. It's not at all the proper title.

Enta is for all ventares and the Chorage have no such word. Choragian has a different word for priest than for priestess, and nothing else. Serzan is not man or woman, is both and neither and changing as befits a river priest, though they have been so since long before they took up the sacred rushes.

Xyrma dips his head. "So you are leaving?" he says, nearly friendly.

They hate him. Him and all the new priests, with their interloper gods of growing fruit and ripened gold and not of desert and dust and flood. They hate that he can swim the rivers better than they can as their bones dry and creak with age.

They make to walk past him. He steps to stand politely in their way.

Xyrma says, "You'll be pleased to know I have spoken with the High One on behalf of your traditional faiths."

Serzan stares at him, at the bridge of his nose and not his eyes, as ever.

"You may practice them, alongside ours, with respect," he says, smiling in encouragement. When he spreads his arms his rich robes seem a waterfall. "A civilised understanding."

They blink quickly at his nose, and step past him and walk along. The Huksha flows noisy beside them, familiar brown beloved, and urgency is hooking behind their heart at last, though for what they don't know.

"Enta Serzan, you overstep," he calls after them. It could sound a threat, but he sounds embarrassed.

"I am pleased," Serzan calls back without turning around. "Don't I look pleased?"

There might be some way he can stop them, by praying to his god of furnace and fury, or reporting at once to his High One. He doesn't, yet.

Serzan walks on alone. It's a long walk, to the coast. Perhaps they'll enjoy it. It has been many years since their last pilgrimage, and they should love the chance to walk the length of their sacred river.

The Huksha is silent as ever. She has never spoken to them as she did to the priests of ancient times. By the end of half a day Serzan has blisters on their toes and heels, and a worn-through sandal strap.

At least most of the land they pass has not been burned, not like the city. At least that.

No god of the land intervened when the Choragians came and burned and plundered. Kazyani Vash has abandoned them, but there is one seed of hope, one Serzan is too hollow and burned-away to know how to grow: the conquerors did not come by sea.

They sleep that night a little away from the waters, mostly lying open-eyed. When they wake it's with a tired buzz in their brain, and they can get no fish to bite, not for all their coaxing, and after barely a fifth of the morning their sandal strap breaks. It takes until noon to gather and weave reeds to properly replace it.

But it holds. Serzan finds their stride. They've fasted for longer than this, and the blisters can hardly hurt worse than they do already. "I'm not as old as that," Serzan says aloud. The Huksha flows beside them, unconvinced.

The next day, there is fish, and they cook it with their grains for a porridge which they eat again that night and the next morning.

The landscape changes as they travel down the Huksha. Untended trees as well as the farmer-planted figs, less cattle and more goats as the country gets rocky and restless from nearness to the sea.

They've gone two days without food when they approach where the river flows into her mother the ocean, weaving through hills that rise high on either side. Long-legged birds stalk and call.

A few modest cattle graze on one hill. Serzan hikes up.

A farmer stands by a fence post with a hammer in one hand. To judge by her clothes and cattle she's well-off for her caste. At their approach she turns, her eyes guarded. "Enta?"

Serzan touches their fingers to their wrists, enough of a greeting. "I need a sacrifice."

The farmer's shoulders tense. "I have no children still to take," she says. When Serzan says nothing, she takes a step back. "The fight took them."

She confuses Kazyani Vash with Arca. "One of your herd will do well," Serzan says, too tired to sound kind.

Hammer dangling, she stares at them.

Five head of cattle, with one strong bull among them. If she has more land than just this hill, she has pitifully few hands left to tend it, robbed like all Arcatan, like Serzan. And she's taking too long for the husk that's left of their patience. "Never mind it," they say, walking past her.

They sleep tucked among rocks that night, close enough to hear the crash of waves. On some level they're delaying the conversation they've walked all this way to have, unsure how much the lady Kazyani Vash will take. But by the sea they sleep easy and sweet, and rise almost smiling.

Though Serzan gives voice to the river, it's the sea they worship, all storm and salt. In the morning light she's blue as lapis, flat and endless, all the roundness ringing the world.

They wade forward. The water that laps around their feet seems gentle, though the sea won't care about Serzan one way or another. They wade in over their knees, the waves splashing up to their waist, and here they take off their bag and drop their supplies away into the sea. Everything, except their fishing line and hook.

They slice the hook through the pad of their thumb and dip their hand under, blood spilling into sea. Then they bow into the waters and lift their head again blinking with water streaming down.

"Kazyani Vash," they say, "great lady sea, please let me speak with you."

They wade back and wait.

After a minute their blood has slowed to drips and dribbles, and there is no answer. They wade back in to the waist and ready the hook over their arm.

"Enough, daughter," says the sea, rising, rising: waves build up, lapis-bright, winged like gryphons.

And it feels like a slap. This shouldn't be what matters, but it does. Serzan swallows, for the salt on their tongue tastes like hopelessness. "Great lady, I'm not your daughter."

The wave curling forward trembles like the brink of disaster, but it does not fall, they are not crushed. "Child," says Kazyani Vash, instead. "Peace." One finger of her hand lifts and comes down. A mile away, waves crash mighty against the coast. Serzan can see the curtain of spray, a column in the air. "You're all so small."

Her form is twenty times again a person's size, though this can only be one part of her, she who is all of the sea that circles the world. Her hair is long and winding and trails merging into the rest of the water. She has one eye in the centre of her face. All Arcatan is her other eye, cradled in her hair.

Serzan has believed in her like something burrowed deep in their lungs all their life, and they have never seen her before. "Great lady, thank you." They should feel more strange and wondrous here. Too much foul has happened, perhaps.

The hair of Kazyani Vash curls, twists, endlessly moving and staying the same. "Speak. Tell me your troubles. But they must be worth something, for it is not wise to bore me."

They bow again, not as deep. She said to speak so they shall speak. "It is the invaders that trouble me," Serzan says, to the bridge of her nose and not her great swirling eye. "I speak for the river they poison."

Kazyani Vash says nothing, not in her voice like a human voice, not with the crash of waves or the scream of gulls, not with sharks come to tear at their legs. There are so many ways to be killed by the sea.

It feels surely the ground will give way before them, the footing unsteady. Serzan keeps going. "These Choragians, their priests know nothing of soil or holy things. They farm the land every year, not letting it lie farrow. They make no pilgrimage."

Against years of habit, it's her eye their gaze is drawn to, the constant eddying swirl. She says, "Dirt is nothing to me."

Can gods laugh? At mortals, yes. Serzan flounders. "But your daughters," they say. "Your tributaries. Huksha and Rey-Ran-Rey and Gaa. All are poisoned, yoked by poor custodians. It is not just the people."

At least there will have been this. If nothing else, at least this. Serzan is lower than the worm the fish eats, for the sight of their god is not enough to make any of this worthwhile. They could never do enough. They cannot make her see, do not deserve her aid. Kazyani Vash, looking down at them as her waters push playful at their knees, Kazyani Vash kind, beautiful, cruel.

"We're dying," Serzan says. "You must care!"

All along the coast, her waters eat away at Arcatan's rocks, even as they support and cradle them. Her head drops closer to Serzan, hair twisting like thick snakes. Her great voice is a murmur. "Why should I, child?"

And Serzan looks at her and says, "You're all I have left."

And they know it's not enough reason. Deep down they know with certainty that all is as dark as it seems, and as terrible.

"I know this," Kazyani Vash says. "Your devotion fills your heart."

Guilt burns their brow like a coal, and they don't say that it's because there's nothing else there.

"I would give you anything," Serzan says. "My life, if you want it."

The swirl of her eye is unreadable, it sucks them in. "Child," she says. "You already have."

So they have nothing of worth left to give her. "You do me great honour just to come," Serzan says, hardly able to lift their voice from a mumble.

The waters rise around them, and lift them. The water's still only up to their waist but they are suspended, like a gnat caught in a hailstone: gripped in the fist of a wave, about to be flung violently down—but they are held, still and safe.

"I can burn them away," Kazyani Vash says.

They would flinch, were they not so tired. Better they naysay a god than Latzamu take another burning. "No, great lady."

"I can sweep you away," she says, the waters tightening around them.

"Yes, great lady," Serzan says. Of course she can.

"I can sweep them away," says Kazyani Vash, and they find her eye, through the twists of water, and don't know how to find their thanks.

"O, greatest one," they say, bowing their head. "O, great and bitter sea."

She sets Serzan down and their feet find the sand, toes digging into it familiar. She still towers above them, familiar too and awful and strange.

"Will you swear on your blood to serve me?" she says. "I, and only I of all of us?"

A dangerous promise. There are many gods. "Lady," they say hoarse, without a moment's thought. "I've served you all my life."

"Enta Serzan," Kazyani Vash says, and her hair twines all around them. "Be my good left hand."

Nearly like joy it overcomes them. "Yes!"

Her strands of hair swirl away, return, a thousand patterns, the waves lifting and falling. "The next great flood but one will wash them away," Kazyani Vash says. The towering figure takes a step back into the deeps. "Warn your people."

There are more Choragian folk in Latzamu than just soldiers now. Children and peaceful folk and priests. A part of Serzan wants to leave them all to burn. They've served the lady of waters all their life but all they want is to walk into ashes.

They wonder, while wishing they didn't, why Xyrma can't grow the beard his faith demands. He claimed to have spoken on their behalf to his leader, in his own way he was trying to help. The dim pang of conscience is a fish-scale cutting through their thumb. Kazyani Vash is turning away.

Serzan lifts their voice higher. "I will evacuate all," they call. "I'll leave no one to the merciless tides, but I will tell the Choragians this is the holy speaking of our gods, that they must leave."

For a moment, her head is sharp in profile, then she turns to them. "If you like," says Kazyani Vash. The toss of her hair could be mistaken for playful. "If you wish to do bad service."

They wade a step after her. They would wade willing into the endless seas. "I want nothing but to serve you."

"You want nothing," Kazyani Vash says.

Serzan goes pale, to be so known.

She reaches down a hand to touch them square on the forehead. "Have hope."

They wake up washed by a wave onto dry and stubbled sand. They press the palms of their hands to the ground. They breathe in deep of the morning calling of the birds, though they do not smile.

On the two-week walk back home, they catch fish each morning with the first line they throw, as though the waters were clean.

About the Author:

Rem Wigmore, also published under Summer Wigmore, is a speculative fiction writer based in Wellington. Their first novel 'The Wind City' *was published in 2013 by Steam Press, and their stories appear in the* 'Sharp & Sugar Tooth' *anthology and the* 'Capricious Gender Diverse Pronouns Issue'. *Rem likes coffee, friendship, and fighting capitalism. They can be found on twitter as @faewriter.*

STRANDED

Stephen Herczeg

The *Valentine* pushed on through the seas, dragging the massive trawl net along the bottom many fathoms below. She was a trawler out of Port Lincoln, a sprawling city that had grown on the back of the fishing industry for well over a century, providing a gateway to all the Southern Ocean had to offer. She was a factory ship. Whatever came up in the nets was processed, packed away and frozen for transport back to land within hours of being caught. Her hold was almost ninety percent full. Another two days and they would head back to port. The crew was relieved. These trips were profitable but hard work during the day and damn boring at night.

Murphy checked the strain on the net. It was almost at capacity. "Net coming up," he called into his microphone. The message blared across the boat. Every man ran to their predefined positions in anticipation.

They had to get the net up and emptied quickly. Any delay in processing and packing the fish would mean more time at sea. Spoilt product would be dumped, which meant a drop in profits. The crew were mostly after toothfish, prawns and crayfish, anything that lived on the ocean floor. Captain Sommers didn't care, it was all fish to him. The company didn't care, there was a market for anything these days, as long as it was fresh.

Murphy admitted that the money was the only reason he was here. The same as most of the others. He wasn't so sure about the Captain though.

When everyone was ready, he activated the winch. The great steel wheels turned and hauled in the thick cables. Within a couple of minutes, the top part of the nylon rope net appeared on the stern ramp.

Even from his position on the bridge, Murphy heard the grinding noise as the winches struggled to haul the catch in. "Jesus, we've hit the motherlode," he said to Turner, the first mate, standing nearby.

"Ain't gonna snap, are they?" Turner asked, eyeing the winches.

"Should be fine," said Murphy, a small nugget of fear rising in his gullet. "I better get out there and check the tension up close." He headed out of the wheelhouse and climbed down a gangway to the main deck. The huge wheels of the winch struggled on, the grinding noise beginning to peter out as they overcame the weight of the net.

Thank God for that.

Murphy looked towards the stern and saw the first of the fish that had been snagged in the net. They were mostly toothfish mixed with southern krill. Either breed was worth its weight in gold. Given the strain on the winches, that weight was enormous. Dollar signs flashed before Murphy's eyes at the thought.

After this I might be able to take a year off.

Finally, the entire net bulging with wriggling fish and crustaceans was brought up from the ice-cold sea.

Murphy stopped the winches and flicked another switch that picked the net up and dangled it above the deck of the ship.

Thompson moved below the net and unlatched the interleaved hatches built into the deck, revealing a gaping maw within the middle of the ship. Pete Howard stepped up to the net and pulled on the bright blue securing line. The net split open at the bottom and a steady stream of fish and krill spilled out into the processing plant below.

And then it happened.

A bright orange and purple form dropped from the net. Eight tentacles shot out at every angle. They tensed across the opening and held the massive bulbous head in place for a moment before it slithered to one side and away from the opening.

Murphy immediately saw that it was a giant ocean octopus. Incredibly rare. This one was much larger than anything Murphy had read about; they generally grew to a length of about three metres. This one was almost six from head to the tip of its tentacles.

It slithered across the deck, following the water flowing out of the open stern. Then it did something unexpected.

It stopped.

Its baleful eyes peered around and focused on the men surrounding it. It sat on the deck, its head expanding and contracting as if the thing was catching its breath or thinking about its next move.

A tentacle shot out and slapped Smith away. He slammed into the side railing and dropped to the deck, sliding several metres towards the stern before laying still.

"Holy crap," came a call from one of the men.

That grabbed the creature's attention. Another tentacle shot and out coiled around the man before he could move away. He cried out in pain as a spray of blood erupted from his mouth. Murphy heard the man's ribs crack and saw the tentacle bulge as it flexed and squeezed the life from his shipmate. Finally, it tossed him away and he slid across the deck and out through the ramp. Murphy watched him bob in the dark waves for a moment before he was swept away.

The rest of the men fled in a blind panic. Nobody knew what to do, and no one wanted to take the lead. Several men dived into the opening in the deck. One was caught before he could disappear from view. The octopus simply retracted its tentacle and tossed the screaming man overboard.

Murphy unconsciously checked his lifejacket. If he ended up in the water, he wanted some protection. He peered out from behind the crane and spied several gaffing sticks tucked away under the port railing.

Sliding across the slick deck, he pulled a gaff loose and turned to face the beast. It stared back at Murphy, transfixing him with the depths of its huge saucer-shaped eyes. A tentacle lashed out towards him.

He knocked it away before it could close around him and stepped forward, swinging the gaff around like a baseball bat.

The barbed hook slammed into one of the thing's eyes, which exploded in a pool of thick viscous goo. Instinctively, its tentacles grabbed at the gaff pole, tearing it free and making a worse mess of its eye.

Murphy turned and grabbed another gaff with a straight barbed head. Steadying himself for a moment, he threw it spear-like straight between the octopus' eyes.

His throw was true. The monster writhed in agony as the spear buried itself deep into its brain. Tentacles squirmed and thrashed as the beast struggled to free the spear. It finally tore it loose, ripping a great hunk of flesh from itself and loosing a torrent of fluid.

The two tentacles grasping the spear dropped to the deck and lay still. The pole rolled towards Murphy. He picked it up quickly and stepped forward. A tentacle twitched making him jump back. Resolve washed over him and he drove the gaff deep into the creature's brain. Grunting with the effort but feeling an inner need to finish the monster from the deep.

All movement stopped.

The baleful eyes lost their glint and glazed over. The tentacles stopped twitching and the head deflated. It was over.

Murphy stared at the hulking carcass. Part of him felt a twinge of pity. The beast's presence here was an accident. The ship was in its home and its reaction was only natural. Murphy wished it had simply taken a flight instinct instead of fight. All would have been far better off. An inner feeling of self-preservation overrode his admiration for the creature.

Captain Sommers stepped up next to him. "Well done, Murphy. Can we take that thing with us?"

Murphy shook his head. "Too tough. People like their octopus to be tender, not battle-hardened leather like this. We could take it back to study."

"Bugger that, it'll take up too much space in the freezer. Best throw it back. All right then," the Captain said, stepping past Murphy and organising a team of men to rid the *Valentine* of the creature's body.

Murphy watched and hoped that was the last he'd ever see of the creature or anything like it.

The squall came out of nowhere.

Murphy was alone in the wheelhouse, poring over maps of the local area to find the best sources of fish for the next day's trawling. After the day's events, he wanted to fill the hold as quickly as possible and head back to land. He'd spent most of the afternoon helping find the men lost overboard and assisting those who had been injured. His mind still reeled from the black orbs of the octopus staring through him.

"Time for a career change," he said under his breath.

The winds hit the ship, snatching at the loose chains and ropes outside. Waves rocked the vessel as the swell picked up.

Murphy stepped out of the cabin and watched the black clouds groping their way over the horizon towards the stern.

The Captain strode out of the galley and stared out at the maelstrom. "What in blazes?" he yelled. He turned and saw Murphy on the deck above. "Murphy, where did this come from? Why were there no warnings?" he shouted.

Murphy kicked himself internally.

The radar. Surely it was on the radar.

He ducked back into the cabin and put his face over the radar's viewfinder. It was clear. The storm wasn't showing on the scope. He pulled away and looked back out to sea.

Impossible.

Murphy strode back out and shouted to the Captain. "It's not on the radar. I can't tell how big it is."

The Captain's curses were lost in the wind. He turned and shouted orders to all and sundry. Sailors and deck hands ran across the deck, lashing anything that was loose in place, securing anything that looked like it could be lost in the approaching storm.

Turner joined in, barking orders at anybody near enough to hear him. As they moved around the deck, the sailors paused and stared out at the approaching tumult. Lightning cast brief flashes of radiance across the face of the black clouds as it arced across the storm. Every man stared up at the closing storm with wide eyes and the haunted look of their approaching mortality. These weren't the type of conditions that anyone wished to face when thousands of miles away from land.

The Captain lurched across the rolling deck and made it to the gangway leading up to the bridge. He brushed past Murphy and headed inside.

He reached the wheel and turned to starboard. The great ship reacted as expected, slowly. Waves stirred up by the storm lashed the ship's port side as it veered away, travelling in a wide arc towards a small rocky outcrop visible in the failing light. An island.

Murphy stepped out of the cabin to check on the rest of the crew. The sky had darkened dramatically as the clouds rolled in. The wind whipped up white caps on the black waves as they reared up and broke over the side of the ship.

The *Valentine* lurched, throwing Murphy onto his back. A wave crashed over the side and washed him onto the deck. His breath left him as he landed heavily and slid across the surface, hitting his head on the edge of the centre hatch.

He sat up slowly, holding his head and trying to clear his vision. The other men were grasping onto anything to keep themselves upright as even larger waves crashed across the ship.

Murphy crawled across to the side rail and dragged himself to his feet. He grabbed the railing just as a large wave struck, rocking the boat to starboard.

Two crewmen screamed as they were swept overboard. Murphy was sure they had thick orange ropes tied around their waists. He shook his head and put it down to the knock he'd received.

He tried to make his way back to the gangway. The main deck was too dangerous, his best bet was back in the cabin with the Captain.

Just as he reached for the stair-rail another massive wave smashed into the ship and Murphy was lifted with the surge and thrown overboard, landing in the midst of the broiling sea.

He turned and looked back. Waves crashed into the side of the trawler and the wind drove her towards the little rocky outcrop the Captain had seen.

Murphy searched for other survivors in the water around him but couldn't see any further than a few feet. Waves tossed him around like a floating cork, making any progress impossible. He concentrated on just staying afloat long enough until the seas calmed down so he could swim towards the island.

His plan worked until another immense wave picked him up and dumped him straight on top of a large piece of floating timber. His head smacked into the wood, and darkness claimed him.

Murphy awoke to excruciating pain. A scream formed on his lips but the chill cry of terror he heard, came from another.

A figure ran away from the shore.

Benson?

Trailing behind him at incredible speed was a long slender tentacle. Similar to the creature's caught up in the *Valentine's* net, but thicker and stronger. The moonlight glinted off the outer skin as it caught up with Benson and lashed out, curling itself around his legs and bringing him down to the sand.

The tentacle withdrew into the water, dragging the screaming sailor with it. Near the water's edge, he was lifted high into the sky and the tentacle released him, allowing him to fall back towards the hard-packed sand near the shore.

Benson's neck let out a splintering crack as he fell headfirst into the sand. He lay still and the tentacle moved on to its next prey.

Small mounds dotted the shoreline. Murphy realised these were the bodies of his other ship mates, stunned, killed and left for dead by the owner of the tentacle.

With his attention diverted, the pain returned. Murphy looked down: he was sitting on a thick upper branch of a tree. His leg was impaled on a small branch growing vertically out of his perch. Blood trickled down to pool amongst the roots. He wanted to scream, to wail, but self-preservation held his tongue.

Cries echoed across the beach as more of Murphy's ship mates succumbed to Benson's fate. He peered into the fading night but could only see shadows. He needed daylight.

After an agonising wait, the first light of dawn broke. Murphy saw a tentacle drag another man towards the water and dash his body into the nearby rocks. As the sun shone across the tentacle it quickly disappeared amongst the gentle waves and all was once again still.

Murphy surmised that he had until night to find shelter and safety.

His attention turned to his impaled limb. The branch was smaller than he'd first imagined. Its jagged end, painted red with his blood, pointed straight up. He shuffled slightly trying to get a better look. The pain lancing through the limb, as the flesh twisted around the stick, stopped him quickly.

He could see that the branch had speared through the meaty underside of the thigh. Blood seeped from the wound, soaking his trousers, but wasn't pouring out. He presumed that meant it hadn't nicked an artery only muscle.

Shouldn't need a parrot or a peg leg then.

Murphy needed to get down. He gritted his teeth and pulled his leg from the protruding tree branch. His resolve finally failed, and he screamed his throat raw. He passed out and fell from his perch.

He awoke on the ground with a throbbing pain in his head to match the agony in his leg and gingerly sat up to examine the wound. It wasn't as bad as he had thought but was leaking copious amounts of blood.

He tore his shirt into strips and bound the wound, staunching the blood and dulling the pain. He looked around and could see bodies scattered across the sand leading all the way to the desolate hulk of the ship that lay dashed upon the nearby rocks.

The ship. I gotta get to the ship. The lifeboat might be fine.

But the night hid an evil that may return, and his immediate concern was to find a safe haven to hide from the creature's tentacles.

Murphy carefully hauled himself up the tree-trunk, his body shaking with the effort. Sweat burst out all over, but he managed to gain his feet. He ripped a branch from the tree to use as a crutch and set off to explore the immediate area.

Thoughts of duty crowded his mind, dictating his initial goal to check on any nearby bodies. A small part of him said that some of his comrades could still be alive.

The first body was his erstwhile companion of many adventures, Turner, food for the rats now. Murphy said a silent prayer, more for himself than Turner, before searching the body for the Armory keys. After many years working the Indian Ocean, Captain Sommers took piracy seriously and insisted that a small number of firearms be stored on the ship, just in case.

The gaff had killed the smaller creature. A gun may not work, but it would provide a level of comfort.

As he staggered on, he came to a path that led to the interior of the island. He followed it to investigate his new-found home but was immediately disappointed when he crested a nearby dune and found another sandy beach. The island was extremely narrow and peering towards both ends of the beach, he saw it wasn't very long either. The low brush and few trees did not present adequate protection from the sea creature if it was to return.

Murphy needed the security of the ship and the added benefit of the stores and weapons it held. He turned and headed back towards it.

The sun rose higher as he continued his shaky journey of only fifty yards. His leg was on fire and a band played a tattoo in his head. He reached the beach and turned towards the ship. Every few yards heralded yet another dead comrade. Expressions of pain, fear and disbelief were writ large on their lifeless faces.

The final body was Captain Sommers. His crumpled form and relative wholeness evidence that he had been thrown from the ship as it hit rather than succumbed to the dark entity of the night. Murphy bowed his head in goodbye and looked up at the great hulk of the once proud *Valentine*.

The storm had driven her ashore and plunged her starboard side onto the jagged rocks of this desolate island. As Murphy stared, he saw hope and a new object of his quest. The starboard lifeboat was still attached, he hoped the port side boat remained intact also. He could lower it straight into the water if it was.

As he reached the side of the ship, and readied to climb the starboard ladder, he noticed large circular marks on the side of the hull. Each was over a foot in diameter and a line of them ran almost parallel to the ladder itself.

The climb up the ladder left his mind reeling and his body staggering on the verge of collapse. The deck was clear of life but a multitude of deep marks across the surface indicated the listing hulk had received a visitor during the night. Any crew members he hadn't seen on the beach were likely deep within Davy Jones' locker providing food for the fish.

Murphy staggered across to the port side and, with relief, found the lifeboat intact and ready to be lowered. He swayed across to the galley to procure what provisions he could. Food, water, fresh clothes, rope and weapons made their way into the lifeboat. His last visit was to the bridge.

His pessimism grew at the sight of the equipment. The cabin windows had been smashed and the bridge flooded by the storm's waves. All equipment had shorted out in the torrent. The radio was dead, along with every other electronic device.

Out of loyalty, Murphy gathered up the ship's paper log. The Captain regularly added his daily accounts to the journal and Murphy decided it was a way of preserving his shipmates' legacy if handed over to the proper authorities.

The pain reached blinding levels and forced Murphy to his knees where he evacuated his stomach across the polished wooden floorboards of the bridge. He doubted that the Captain would care anymore, but it left him with a sense of betrayal, which vanished when he fell to the floor and passed out.

Murphy slept through the rest of the day only to stir later that evening. His fevered mind imagined horrors of huge tentacles slithering across the ship's deck and their suckers attaching themselves to the door attempting to gain entry to the cabin where he reposed.

He finally woke and sat up for a moment to gather his thoughts. Moonlight streamed into the cabin through the stern windows. On unsteady feet, he moved over to them and peered out across the beach below.

His mouth dropped open in utter shock.

Down below on the beach, the creature had returned, and it had been busy. All of his crew mates' bodies had been gathered together and piled in an untidy heap at the edge of the shore. Several of the creature's tentacles were whipping and writing across the beach, bringing the final bodies to the water's edge and dumping them on the heap.

The tentacles withdrew and moments later the calm sea just off the beach began to bubble and froth. A great domed mound of smooth skin rose through the tumult until it sat several feet above the water's surface. The bright moon shone off the dome and lit the surrounding water. Dark baleful eyes, gigantic versions of those possessed by the smaller beast Murphy had slain, poked above the water line and stared at the pile of bodies.

The giant monster was joined by smaller versions on either side. It wasn't alone but part of a family group. Murphy almost screamed at the thought that such leviathans existed in this world. He maintained his calm, knowing full well that to shout out would be his death.

Suddenly, huge tentacles reached out from below the roiling sea and stretched towards the pile of bodies. They belonged to the middle creature: the patriarch. Its tentacles picked up one of the dead sailors' bodies and brought it to eye level.

It's looking at the bodies?

When finished, it tossed the body aside. The other great creatures' tentacles flashed across the water and grabbed at the corpse. The creatures fought for possession, ripping the sailor apart with incredible strength.

Once claimed, the remaining parts were taken below the waterline, which soon became a foaming spume of water that turned red within moments.

After only a few minutes, the pile of bodies had almost disappeared. Each of the titanic creatures was treated to a flow of Murphy's shipmates, but the central beast seemed to take on an agitated manor.

It's searching for something, or someone.

In his mind's eyes he saw the vision of the smaller octopus. Its dark obsidian eyes staring into his own, burrowing deep into his soul.

Had it cast that sight to the leader of its clan? Am I its target? I'm dead if I stay here. Gotta get to land.

He shifted his weight. A bolt of pain from his leg told him that he was in no shape to take action yet. He grimaced, lay down under the nearby console and let sleep claim him once again until morning.

Dawn streamed into the cabin when Murphy awoke. He staggered to the stern windows and saw the beach vacant of bodies and of the gigantic titans of the deep. Outside, the deck was clear, and the port side lifeboat unmolested.

He staggered to the boat and lowered it.

He managed to climb down and into the boat without fainting again, took two pain tablets from the first aid kit and wolfed them down with sips of precious water.

He hacked at the ropes to set the boat free and rowed north, keeping the rising sun on his left but heading as far away from the death ship *Valentine* as he could. He silently prayed he was headed towards safety.

The painkillers, the action of rowing for several hours, and the sun beating down on him, overrode the cold chill of the air and drove him back to slumber. A pale twilight of another night greeted him as he awoke again.

Murphy looked to the stars and kept the Southern Cross before his sight as he continued to row. His strokes became timid at best as his strength was almost completely drained. He rested and observed the serenity of the open sea. No bird squeals could be heard and only the gentle lapping of the waves against the lifeboat's hull greeted him in the dark starlit night.

Murphy looked back the way he'd come, but his constant rowing had managed to put the island far to the south and well over the horizon. There was nothing to be seen, just ocean all around.

For the first time in many hours, Murphy finally felt safe.

Suddenly, there was a splash far off in the water. A moment later, something slapped against the hull.

About the Author:

Stephen is an IT Geek, writer, actor, film maker and Taekwondo Black Belt based in Canberra Australia. He has been writing for over twenty years and has completed a couple of dodgy novels, sixteen feature length screenplays and dozens of short stories and scripts.

Stephen's scripts, 'TITAN', 'Dark are the Woods', 'Control' and 'Death Spores' have found success in international screenwriting competitions with a win, two runner-up and two top ten finishes.
His horror stories have featured in various anthologies including: Sproutlings; Hells Bells; Trickster's Treats #1, #2 and #3; Shades of Santa; Below the Stairs; Behind the Mask; Beyond the Infinite; Beside the Seaside; The Body Horror Book; Anemone Enemy; Petrified Punks; Beginnings; Sea of Secrets, Demonic Carnival; Deep Space; A Tribute to H.G. Wells; What If?; Through Death's Door and Coffins and Dragons.

Over forty of his drabbles have been accepted by Blood Song Books; Black Hare Press; Fantasia Divinity and ThingsInTheWell.

Several of his Sherlock Holmes pastiches have been accepted for inclusion in anthologies published by Belanger Books and MX Publishing.

You can catch Stephen at his Facebook page:
https://www.facebook.com/stephenherczegauthor

A TWISTED TAIL

Zoey Xolton

Serena revelled as the cool, salt-water spray surged up from the surf to alight on the breeze, sprinkling her in crystalline droplets. She sighed. She had lived a long and fruitful human life, and now, more than anything—she longed to return to the waves.

She missed her family beneath the sea; her parents, sisters, and friends.

Dare she step into the water and allow herself to melt into sea foam? *A life without a tail, is no life at all,* she decided. With courage, she went forth . . .

And regained her tail and youth!

Serena gasped in the shallows as she beheld her beautiful, original form. *The sea witch lied!* "So, that bitch thought she could keep me from reclaiming my kingdom? Tricked me into believing I'd sacrificed my immortality . . ." Diving into the deep blue, she smiled darkly. "The queen is coming home,

Ulana, and unfortunately for you, the humans have taught me a thing or two about playing dirty!"

About the Author:

Zoey Xolton is an Australian Speculative Fiction writer, primarily of Dark Fantasy, Paranormal Romance, and Horror. Her works have appeared in over one-hundred themed anthologies, with more due for publication!

She has recently celebrated the release of her debut short story collection Darkly Ever After. *You can find further details regarding her many publications on her website: www.zoeyxolton.com!*

Scales and Sand and Sorrow

Rebecca Dale

He was right about me. That's what hurt the most.

Here I was, a hair's chasm away from the most clichéd suicide in the world and all I could think was that he'd been right about everything.

I laughed and looked over the city as the sun set. New York was the place where dreams came to die, and maybe if I ended here, I was some semblance of a dream too. The kind of dream you forget, perhaps. Running in the forest. Drowning. A blurred smile. Something tired and well worn. That was alright.

At the top of the Empire State is an ocean. Horns and engines and the shifting of concrete come together. The sounds of New York coalesce and cadence into waves. It is unspeakably peaceful.

I crammed myself between warm bodies, strung together by errant scarves and coat tails. Couples brought their heads together to talk in whispers. My breaths shallowed. I stood still with my head bowed and waited.

And then the throng parted, pulled by the gravitation of the earth and my own fate. I stepped into it, letting the New York summer leave its bitter taste on the back of my tongue. I slipped beside a set of coin-operated binoculars. There was bile in my throat as I steadied my foot against the stone and wrapped my fingers around the metal lattice.

Nobody noticed. Or maybe they didn't care. Isn't it strange how much Americans talk to each other in elevators but not in crowds? The grate hurt my hands. Obviously it was designed to prevent someone like me doing something very stupid.

I'm not stupid, I'd said once, and without a pause he'd turned his head, big blue eyes burning into mine, the question coming out of him slow and quiet.

Aren't you?

I shook my head because that was over now. Fear knotted up my stomach and I swallowed it down as I climbed. The hands, at least, were strong. They knew cold tiles and the precise texture of blood and how to get back up again and how to pull, pull, pull.

But my limbs paused at the precipice. The ocean sound crashed over me and the lights of the city glimmered like glowing microbes. My knees and thighs spasmed from the awkwardness of the climb. Almost over the edge and down, down, down and I didn't dare to look. It was okay. It was okay. I looked to the sky instead.

And I saw something wrong, cut from the other cloth of the universe.

There are ancient responses to such sightings. Not flight, not fight, but freeze. The brain knows, at the back where the medulla sits, when it beholds something that is not meant to be seen. A primordial freezing took hold of me. I was the ancient rabbit caught in the headlights.

Eyes and fins and scales and starlight. It loomed over me, monstrous and beautiful. A first I thought it was a blimp burning to the ground. But the movement was too wrong and too elegant.

It drifted in front of me, its eyes glistening, pushing forward. As it draws near my hand, clutching the top of the rail recoils backwards. But it persists until my open hand is full. The gentlest nudge, cold and slick and wet, urges me backwards.

And as I fall, there is release. The endless chanting in my head—*stupid, stupid, meaningless, worthless, stupid*—softens and quietens.

Strong hands catch me and turn me on the floor. An attendant dressed in a crisp scarlet uniform and a bell-boy cap shakes my shoulders. His eyes are frantic and wide as leans over me.

"What are you doing?" he screams, "are you stupid? *Are you?*"

Maybe I am. And maybe I'm also crazy, exactly like he said, because when I close my eyes the dreams are the same as always, except the blood is water, and the whisk of a gold fin fans the rivulets away from me.

The phone rang. I put it down on the pillow and stared at the screen until my eyes hurt.

Children thumped down the hall beyond the hotel room door. I wanted to go out there, with the veins in my temple building, and demand their silence. But I hadn't left this bed in three days. I hate hotel rooms, but I can't go back to that apartment on Statton Island, where the heat slides over my skin and leaves residue.

My head pounded as the air conditioning unit near the window blasted icy air into the room. I reach for it again but fall quiveringly short. All the strength I have left is preserved in my fingers, resevoired into simple acts; plugging in the phone when the battery gives out, pulling it back to my chest, tapping at the screen until it pressing the ringer button.

How many times had I pressed it, only for the call to ring out? I've lost count.

That thought filled my chest with tightness and frayed nerve endings. My heart *literally* hurts. I imagine him looking at my name as his phone rings, as he swipes the call away. And at least he thinks of me. If nothing else. He will not speak to me. But this ritual is better than nothingness.

A click.

"I'm recording this conversation," he says.

My haze of nightmares and firm pillows dissolves. His voice is quiet and firm. My fingers fumble and the phone drops to the floor. When I pick it up, a shattered screen scatters the display, breaks up his name into ancient symbols.

I couldn't remember what I was saying. The words left my lips and were gone forever, even though their internal workings were the same. They were words of begging, and weeping, and confusion. Pleas given at a disinterested temple.

But every word of his singes the delicate skin of my eardrums and is intoned there forever.

It's not my fault, he said. You've changed, he said. You used to be a free spirit.

But then you wanted me to be somebody I'm not. You wanted every part of my life to belong to you.

You made every little thing an explosion.

Like the goldfish. It was just a mistake. I forgot. People make mistakes. But you cried and you cried. Do you know how ugly you are when you cry? You were ridiculous. Sometimes things are broken. It's not anybody's fault.

You just wouldn't stop talking. You were always talking. But none of the words were important.

Like now.

You blame me, but it was your choice to come here. It was your choice to be with me, no matter what. I'm not your knight. And you cried about everything. It was impossible.

You're gaslighting me, do you know that? You keep telling me my actions hurt you. But did they really? Aren't you responsible for your own emotions?

If you had only just left me alone. If only you'd gone away when I told you.

Then this would never have happened to you.

Then those little goldfish would be alive.

In a slow place, I saw it for a second time. There were voices there, distant and fleeting, asking me to stop. There were hands, reaching. They receded away with the tide. It was hard to blink, as if my eyelids were glue. I groaned and tasted the salt spray on the back of my tongue. At first, each step I took was a laboured thing. There was sand beneath my feet, sinking down around my toes.

Reality rushed back over me. Sight and sound pounded at my temples and I wanted to go back there, where it was soft and quiet. Rocks and ocean tempted me, with only the boardwalk of Coney Island behind me, glittering and blaring and all too much. I bolted to the water. Shivers took over me. I gusted along with the wind until the waves closed in.

Further and further I pummelled myself into the foam. My hands clenched and grasped and gripped for a handle on the waves. Salt water burned my lungs and my throat closed itself off against the rising tide. Only my constant coughing ensured that I was still pulling breath. But I wanted it that way. This was good. I swallowed down the acid rising in my stomach. I expected the beach to be dirtier, poisoned like the Hudson. But there was none of the havoc of New York City here. Just the rolling clouds above me ghosting over the setting sun, splaying shades of rose quartz and blue tourmaline. There was peace and stillness and the kindest kind of momentum. I spiralled in. It was okay. It was okay. It was okay.

No-one tells you about the warmth. How it feels when you finally let yourself think about letting go. I closed my eyes and thought about a little golden bed of light where you put your head down and just stop. I don't know when I started thinking about that place. I don't know when I started looking for it. But the water was warm, gliding over my skin. It pulled me in and pushed the world further away. I was wrong to search upwards. This was it, this was so much closer than that night at the Empire State.

Soon I was weightless, both floating and sinking. The cold fell away. Goodbye, goodbye. It didn't hurt and it hurt a lot. My lungs screamed. The back of my head tilted backwards and backwards, as if it was trying to adhere itself to the backs of my shoulders. My eyes forgot how to close. Darkness and stillness surrounded and the endless pinprick of stars. Stars above and below. This was sanctuary. This was a place to rest.

And yet there was movement.

Do you remember when you were a child, and stepping into the ocean, when it happened? Maybe it wasn't your first time. Maybe you'd been in water time after time after time. But then you looked down, and the water was dark and you couldn't quite see, and in the depths there was something. *Something.* Inexplicable. All the calm in you shrivelled away when you realised how wrong you had been, to trust that water. Something reached for you, and even though it only touched your skin for the briefest moment, you recoiled and ran and screamed and never quite trusted again? That moment is yours and mine and belongs to more, a common thread between us.

And there I spun that thread out again, and pulled surrender and slumber back into myself as I realised the darkness was wrong. Something had slipped past me and knocked me off my axis, leaving me tumbling and reeling into starlight.

My arms thrashed of their own accord as *it* approached for the second time, curving around me in a wide arc. Lights danced across its body, its giant tail as thin as a piece of paper, voluminous and liquid and soft. Fins in equal measure billowed out from its body. This was not the sort of being that hurried, its scales and delicate appendages each built from dreams. Each part of it glittered and melded and made one final rupture through the water with its tail. Darkness rushed to fill its wake and pulled me alongside, barrelling me forward until I faced its magnanimous eyes.

I opened my mouth (to scream?) but there was no air left. Instead only the memory of air, tiny bubbles like pearls, spiralling out and leaving my body in all directions.

The eyes are gold, not the silver of whatever faced me in the sky.

And they both won't let me die. They want me to go home.

It drifted over me until its belly was close enough to brush the tip of my upturned nose. Thunder clapped, a dull, horrendous sound that sliced across my skin and it descended. I was smothered in its fins, inhaling scales, its massive body dragging me endlessly down. Or is it up? I don't know anymore.

Nobody likes having two sisters. It leaves you outnumbered.

Why did you stay in the first place? asks the first. It is not a question. Her voice is anger and tightness and trembling sadness.

I love him, I answer. Because even now it is still true.

Get on a place, she says. Just get on a plane. Forget him.

It's not just his fault, I explain. I did things.

None of that matters, says the second. She is stillness. She is the silver moon hovering over the ocean. She is my home town on a Friday night, when the sun has set and the beaches are empty. I can taste the sea spray. It seems like a memory borrowed from somebody else.

Come home, she says, we will take care of you.

But that's worse. Once they set their laser gazes on my ruined body, that's all I'll ever be. I will be a hushed conversation hidden between hands. This worldwide ditch between me and my beautiful sisters will widen to a chasm, their sighs of horror echoing out across the valleys of what's left of me.

They are right. It's incredibly stupid to stay here. This isn't my city. Even the light is wrong. I need the Australian sun. I need to lie down in it and sleep.

But I put down the phone and walk away every time, until my beautiful sisters sob and hang up. Or the phone runs out of power. Whichever is first.

This is not fair on them. Everything that I am. I should go home and face them. They deserve that. When I think that, I realise whatever is holding me is not enough.

But the moment passes, and I linger on.

I don't want to open my eyes. I've adjusted to the void and leaving it behind burns. But soon enough there is sun and wind and water gliding over my body and pushing darkness away. Gravity cannot be denied, it is the only goddess that insists.

There are hands too, pulling me up from the sand. When I swallow I taste salt and stars. But the aftertaste is different somehow: crisper, brighter?

Homelier.

So are the voices that clamour around me. I don't understand how it's possible, how I could have gotten here so quickly. But their faces can't be denied. I find my feet, stand up, teetering precariously as I reach for them. I breath in my sister's hair and smell the geraniums in her garden. Behind me, a second pair of hands laces its fingers with mine, clutching me the same way that they used to, when we were all small, full of giggles, tucked away in a blanket big enough for three little ones.

How can you be here? asks the first. You're in New York. You cannot be here. This is bloody Fairy Meadow.

The only answers I have are laced across my wrists. Red curves littered on top of one another, pressed hard into my skin and leaving eternal impressions. I cannot tell if I cut these myself, in slips of northern darkness, or if they're as fresh as they look. Perhaps it's some kind of reminder.

I don't understand, says the second. But let's get you home. Her eyes are glimmering and gold.

We're all together now, says the first. It'll be okay now. Even if it hurts. We'll be okay.

She's right. I smile and that hurts too.

About the Author:

Rebecca Dale is a writer and librarian. She studied ancient history and archaeology at the University of Sydney before pursuing a masters in Applied Linguistics and a graduate diploma in Library and Information Services. For the last ten years she has been working in public and academic libraries, producing copy for library training, marketing, exhibitions and community engagement. Her last publication was 'The new librarian's roadmap: at the crossroads of expectation and reality' *for the Australian Library Journal. She lives in Sydney with a very adorable and mischievous rabbit. You can follow her on Instagram (IG:* @ladygreysydney*) or at her website* http://www.rebeccadale.com.au

The Untimely Demise of Disco Stu's Goldfish Shoes

Brianna Bullen

Pause video at 5:52. Barely a scream

in the stream, as you can see: the needle threads

seamlessly through skin & capillaries,

pumping a green solution to the crisis

of rising sea levels. Biotechnology transforms

the body, Potterian Gilly Weed: webbed fingers, external

lung filters scarred across the neck,

slovenly tails stalking through water—layered dancing

skin chainmail scaled all seaweed skirts & petticoats.

Others, giant squid or trailing jellyfish sting entrails. Humans

are granted GMO survival

& grants for underwater construction.

Permits for submarines & scuba gear are given
to those who feel poorly equipped (pending Centrelink).
Some, nervous,
have their nervous systems compromised, turned
into tuna & other smaller fish. The bigger mostly-human fish
gobble them without remorse, keeping a few
as pets, memories of goldfish surprisingly long-lived
when it comes to companion-animal ownership & some others
to breed
in farms to kick-start a new type of fish market. Their little
bodies
are cling wrapped for supermarket sale. Others are
immortalised,
wrapped in cellophane for art exhibits. Eat or be eaten—no
guppy gumption,
human-fish DNA clings to incisors & gums.

Fish bowl towns literalised, communities & pods populate
implementing glass walls of territory, pissing-contest castle
props
& compete for prime reef & rock real estate. Mers murmur,
preening & priming
themselves with swiped seaweed. They compete, holding
themselves

to higher standards & in pockets
of surface sun-turned water.

The planet should be renamed 'Ocean' as there is no earth
left, save
for nostalgic remnants of mountains peeking peaks through
the surface. Surviving snow leopards, rosette patterns on stone,
cling on
in Kathmandu, the big cats water averse & proud in their
elevation,
swipe occasionally at silky selkies or coy mers curled as
commas
curious enough to come to the surface, or who have gotten
high puffing puffer fish
with dolphins. For the less developed lungs, oxygen is still a
needed drink.

Humans with the privilege & resources of mobility settle
in the warmth of El Niño, migrating in the cold shift of La
Niña
to their 'summer houses' still in the equatorial current. The
band created turns Ocean
into a cat's eye, seen from space, brown marble bands in the
centre its pupil.
The vitreous humour of this Earth eye isn't funny, full of vitriol

& parties hunting pariah piranha people in the cold outskirts.

We watch the violence—human nature, refusing to change,
or changing for the worst
in their eat-or-be-eaten-&-not-be-fish nature.
Cities inequality shift serpentine, solidifying
anew under water pressure. Bubbles gasp, grasp for the
surface
& then surrender with a pop. They've transplanted their
excesses
into their new conditions, their worst reflected
in the water, no radical shifts in tide
that could save all.

We watch their foibles through our mechanical god's eye,
our underwater technology screening
every mythic conflict in DVDs part aquatic
part biological, from across the galaxy. They are read
internally
in our cosmic dust body players. Ocean glistens
in its Nebula, minty yet edible as a Milky Way
soaked under river brine. We string it up
with its planetary fellows, little snow globe world strings
the latest in intergalactic fashion.
We 'gods' wear galaxies.

About the Author:

Brianna Bullen is a Deakin University PhD creative writing candidate writing about memory in science fiction. She has had work published in journals including LiNQ, Aurealis, Voiceworks, Rabbit, Multiverse: An anthology of international science fiction poetry, *and* Woolf Pack Zine.

She won the 2017 Apollo Bay short story competition and placed second in the 2017 Newcastle Short story competition. Her manuscript was previously a finalist in the 2018 Subbed In Poetry Chapbook competition. In 2018, she was part of Nexus, an Arts Access Victoria collective for artists with mental health recovery lived experience.

The Pisces Experiment

Carolyn Young

Sister Theresa was concerned. Even though she was yet to take her final vows, her dedication to the church was unwavering. She'd sworn to love all of God's creatures, but the sudden influx of babies into the drop-box of the orphanage was disconcerting. It wasn't the volume that bothered her. These sorts of things often came in waves. Several babies at once, then months before another group appeared. But it was the babies themselves that unsettled Sister Theresa.

The bell rang for the third night in a row and she walked with purpose towards the drop box. The sound of the waves breaking on the beach across the road and the smell of salt were familiar, but the shaking of her hands as she reached to open the flap was not. Placing her fingers lightly on the handle she paused, taking a deep breath before pulling it down firmly. She said a quick prayer to the Almighty that this child would not be afflicted, made the sign of the cross over her heart, then drew the bundle towards her.

The infant wriggled against her chest, its fists waving free from its wrappings and gripping her fingers like a vice.

"Shh, dear one. It's okay. You're safe here," she crooned, not daring to look too closely. The child's skin felt cold and damp, so she pulled against her chest to protect it from the cool sea breeze, then hurried towards the heated nursery.

The room was crammed full of cradles, each containing a new arrival. Sister Theresa felt an involuntary shudder as she looked around. Giving a glance over her shoulder to ensure her momentary loss of composure hadn't been observed, she placed the new baby on a towel laid out on the table. Filling a bowl with warm water and picking up a washcloth her heart raced and a bead of sweat rolled down her forehead. Her hands shook as she unwrapped the blanket.

The baby was a girl, with creamy white skin that shimmered in the dimmed light. Her pale hair was barely visible as a fine soft fuzz upon her head. Sister Theresa gently bathed the girl in sections, careful to pat her dry before she became too cold. The baby lay quietly, staring up at her with clear grey eyes, resisting nothing and the nun felt the tension drain from her body. This one wasn't like the rest and she gave praise to the Lord.

"What a beautiful girl you are. I doubt we'll have any trouble finding someone to adopt you," she whispered, rolling her gently onto her tummy to wash her back.

At the sight of the child's back, Sister Theresa let out a gasp of horror. This was another abomination. The work of Satan. She wanted to turn and run from the room, leaving the infant for someone else to attend to, but she had to honour her duty to the church. She gathered the warm cloth, careful to ensure none of her own skin touched the child, took a deep breath and wiped over the scaly back with its prominent dorsal fin.

Once the child was dressed, fed a bottle of warm milk and placed into a freshly prepared cradle, Sister Theresa backed away from the crib. She passed Lila's crib, her gill slits in her neck the only visible malformation. Her webbed hands and feet, hidden beneath her blanket. Rosa, with her legs fused together into the shape of a tail, and Sophie, who was the first person she had ever seen without a belly button, covered from the chest down in scales, both lay nearby. There were over twenty babies. All slightly different to each other but similar just the same.

Taking a seat near the doorway, Sister Theresa spent the next few hours completing her duties. Four hourly feedings, and nappy changes took up most of the night. Despite her best attempts she couldn't rid herself of the urge to run from this place. Away from these babies who were not just physically different but exhibited behaviour so disturbing that she shied away from their touch.

The eeriest part was the silence. Not a sound was ever heard from any of them. Not just tonight. None of them ever cried. And they were cold. Nothing the nuns did altered the temperature of their skin.

At the end of the shift, Sister Theresa was relieved to hand over care of the babies to Sister Mary. Never before had the trainee nun displayed any sense of discomfort. Sister Mary was a natural with the babies but when Sister Theresa showed her the newest arrival, she saw her own terror mirrored in Sister Mary's eyes.

"Does Mother Superior know of the new arrival?" Sister Mary asked.

"Not yet. I'm going to see her now." With a nod, Sister Theresa left the room, relief flooding her body at no longer being near the children.

Her apprehension returned as she approached the room of Mother Superior. Perhaps she would be reprimanded for her lack of compassion. She knew the vows she planned to take in the spring forbid her from rejecting any of God's children, but still she could not help her revulsion. Knocking quietly, she waited, her hands grasped together, for the door to open. She checked her watch, then again a minute later. Unable to stand it, she paced back and forth in the hallway, her stomach churning, legs unsteady.

Mother Superior's face was serene as she appeared in the doorway. Sister Theresa hoped that with time and prayer she would one day feel that same sense of peace, but for now all she felt was turmoil.

"What is it Sister Theresa?"

"Another child has arrived. Just like the others." Her voice shuddered.

A flicker of concern passed over Mother Superior's face before it once again reflected a calm peace. "Thank you for letting me know. I shall pray for her."

"Where do you think they're coming from? These babies?"

"All babies are sent to us from God, to love, protect and care for until we can find suitable homes for them."

"Yes, but these babies . . . I'm not sure they're God's children."

"It is true they are different, but God teaches us not to focus on the differences we see, but to focus on loving each person as an individual with their own strengths and weaknesses."

"I will try to remember that Mother, when I'm caring for the children."

"You are still young, child. Ask our Lord to give you guidance."

Sister Theresa sensed the invitation to leave, but she held back unsure of whether to voice what she was feeling.

"What is it, child? I can feel that there is more you wish to tell me."

"It's hard for me to say, but when I'm with the babies, I feel afraid. As if I'm in the presence of evil. I've prayed for guidance, but with each new baby that arrives I feel it even more."

"Trust that the Lord is guiding you, even when you don't feel it."

Teresa nodded, before turning.

"Know that I'll add you to my prayers tonight. Goodnight Sister Teresa."

"Goodnight Mother and thank you for your guidance.

The next few months brought relief from the influx of babies to the convent. Sister Theresa was still assigned to look after the babies as part of her training before her final vows and she became used to their differences. Each morning the babies changed, exhibiting more fish-like characteristics. The areas of scaling spread, they grew sharp teeth in their pointed jaws, and slits appeared where their necks met their shoulders. They were no longer silent but made a quiet popping noise. One would make a noise, then the others would take turns at popping too. It was as if they were communicating in some strange language. They grew bigger, but they also grew physically weaker.

Their skin remained cold, but also became paler, and they moved less. Soon they stopped accepting the food they were given. They lay in their cribs, becoming quieter, paler and thinner.

A doctor was called and could find no reason for their appearance or their loss of health. Scratching his beard as he left, he'd muttered something about doing research, but even though he was called many times, he had no further insight into the infants and they showed no signs of improvement.

Although she had grown to accept them, Sister Theresa couldn't stop her curiosity over where these babies had come from and how they came to be so different to other babies. As the babies grew weaker, she wondered if knowing where they came from might help her return them to health. This curiosity, she knew, was forbidden in her role. She constantly prayed for the Lord to take her fear away, but no matter how much she prayed it away, it remained.

On the night that the next baby arrived, Sister Theresa wasn't inside the convent. She'd been sent out earlier to assist at a nearby church fete. Her day had been spent selling balloons to children and collecting money for cakes at the bake sale. Cleaning up afterwards had taken longer than expected, so it was dark when she rode her bicycle home.

As she approached the back entrance to the convent, a large black van pulled up. A man wearing a hoodie, pulled low over his face got out of the passenger seat and opened the back door.

Sister Theresa knew she should offer assistance, but since he was near the drop box her curiosity got the better of her. She ducked behind a parked car and watched.

The man glanced around before pulling a bundle from the rear of the van and carrying it towards the drop box. Sister Theresa's hairs rose on the back of her neck. Could this be the person who was delivering the babies?

The van was black, with no special logos on it, but when she squinted, she could read the number plate. PISCES. At least it was easy to remember. The door to the van closed with a bang and Sister Theresa watched while it took off at speed. The squeak of the drop box being opening and the singsong voice of Sister Mary crooning to the baby calmed Sister Theresa's frayed nerves.

The lights in the nursery were burning when she popped her head in to check on the new arrival. She watched on in silence as Sister Mary washed the new baby, dressing her and wrapping her before placing her into her crib.

"Is she like the others?" Sister Theresa whispered, trying hard not to startle Sister Mary.

Sister Mary's eyes glistened with tears as she turned and nodded towards her. "Just like the others when they arrived. This one's missing ears and as she breathes her nostrils press closed."

"And the scales. Does she have them?"

"Yes, both legs and arms completely covered. It's such a shame. I don't understand it."

Sister Theresa paused, not sure whether or not to share what she had seen. "I saw her being dropped off. She came in a black van. They drove off afterwards."

"Could you tell where they came from?"

"No. The van turned left at the corner of Jasper Street but by the time I got there on my bicycle they were gone."

"While you were gone Sila passed away." Sister Mary said, with tears in her eyes. "They're all becoming so weak, I'm worried that more will die. Nothing I do helps them."

"I'm so sorry. I'll pray tonight for her soul. You do think they have souls, don't you? I wish we knew where they were from. It might help us to help them," Sister Theresa said.

"Pray for little Sila's soul. I'm sure she must have one. All of God's creatures have souls. Mother Superior will lead a service for her tomorrow at two."

"I'll see you in chapel tomorrow and I'll pray for you too. I'm on duty before you tomorrow night, I'll come in early to relieve you. Goodnight Sister."

"Goodnight Sister Mary."

That night Sister Theresa tossed and turned. Thoughts of the babies and the strange van filled her mind and when she finally drifted off to sleep her dreams too. PISCES, the number plate had read. What could that mean? In the early hours of the morning she woke, unable to return to sleep. A plan formed in her mind. She would follow the van, but how would she keep up with it on her bicycle? She was rostered on to look after the babies most nights and she doubted Mother Superior would allow her to leave the convent to investigate.

The following morning Sister Mary was pale and withdrawn. Sister Theresa sat with her, holding her hand as tears formed trails down her cheeks. Another baby had died overnight.

"I don't think I'm meant to be a nun," Sister Mary said. "I know I'm supposed to feel compassion for these babies, but they scare me. I felt a sense of relief when this one died, like a piece of evil had left the room. They're creepy. When I'm with them I jump at every noise. They're so quiet. They lie there awake popping to each other. You'll probably think I'm crazy, but I feel like they're talking to each other."

"It's alright Sister Mary, I've felt the same thing. I don't think they're evil, but I'm sure they don't belong here. I just wish I knew where they came from," Sister Theresa said. "I thought the van might have given me a clue when I saw it last night, but the only thing I noticed was the number plate. It said PISCES, but that means nothing to me."

"Pisces? Are you sure?" Sister Mary grew pale.

"I'm positive. Why? Do you know what it means?"

"The Pisces Institute. It's a research facility just out of town. They're supposed to be testing ocean currents, and water pollution levels."

"Do you think they're involved?" Sister Theresa asked.

"They have a good reputation as being ethical, so I doubt it, but if the van said Pisces, that's definitely where it would have come from."

"I'm going to check it out."

"You can't. We're not allowed to leave here without permission," Sister Mary said.

"I'll work something out. Can I swap shifts with you tonight? I'll do your afternoon shift if you'll cover me tonight."

"You know I will, but please be careful. I have a bad feeling about this."

"I will. Thanks. And please don't tell anyone."

"Of course, I won't."

All afternoon Sister Theresa went through the plan in her head. She couldn't wait until her shift finished and she could leave the convent. No more babies died, but many of them looked close to death. Despite her aversion to them, she still felt a sense of responsibility for them and hoped that she would learn something useful.

"Be careful," Sister Mary said as she took over in the nursery. "I'll be praying for you."

Sister Theresa rode her bicycle along the foreshore towards the large building on the hill. Huge gates blocked the entry of the manicured gardens. Puffing from the effort, she hid her bicycle behind a bush, then walked along the boundary of the fence. There were no gaps big enough to fit through, so she returned to her bicycle and hid, waiting in silence.

The night was colder than she'd expected, and she shivered, wrapping her arms around her body. A rumble stirred in the distance and she saw the approach of headlights. She peered through the leaves as the van approached. The gates opened slowly with a creak. She checked the number plate. PISCES. It was definitely the same van. The gates remained open as the van disappeared around the corner and as they started to close, she slipped through the opening, hitching up her long skirt to run through the darkened garden.

The building was old, with bevelled glass in the windows. Bushy shrubs lined the walls and made it easy for her to hide while peering through them. Voices murmured in the distance, muffled by the glass.

She moved around the building, looking into each window until she came to one that was lit with a bright light. The room was lined with large cylinders filled with water, some of the cylinders were empty, but others contained large objects. The curved surfaces made it difficult for her to see what the objects were. She blinked several times to clear her vision then looked again. The cylinders each contained a naked woman. She stepped back in horror. They looked dead, but when she drew the courage to look again, she saw one of them blink, and another changing position.

The opposite wall contained ceiling-high aquariums with some of the largest fish Sister Theresa had ever seen. Microscopes stood on tables around the room, along with other scientific equipment. Labels on the doors of cupboards warned of the danger of mishandling the samples. None of it made sense. As she turned to move to the next window, she noticed a symbol on the wall, a woman and a fish encircled by a mermaid. That was strange.

She moved along the building to the next window. The room was dimly lit, but she was able to make out more rows of cylinders. Smaller ones, containing babies. Mutant babies who shared some features with the women in the previous room and some with the fish from the tanks. Some form of genetic experimentation was being done here. This was wrong. She backed away, heart racing, skin crawling, tears wetting her cheeks.

The voices were closer now and loud enough for her to hear them. "Michael should be back by now. It doesn't take that long to dump a body."

"Relax Carl. I think I just heard his van come through the gates," another voice replied.

"Can't be too careful. They can't be found. I don't want to end up in jail," Carl said.

"We won't. We're just following orders."

"You know the deal. If anyone finds out, we're all going down."

There was a pause. "Then there's something I should tell you. Michael isn't culling the babies. He's dropping them off at the orphanage down the hill. I drove him last night. He put the baby in the drop box, still alive, and then he left."

"What? I told him to kill them, not drop them at the shelter, like kittens. Grab the keys," the voice boomed. "I should have taken care of it myself."

"But they're only babies. Surely they won't be able to link them back to us and they'll be looked after by the nuns."

"You don't understand. I'm not going to prison over this. And we're so close. The babies are getting more and more fish-like. We'll make a fortune if we can produce a mermaid. The unsuccessful attempts have to die."

Sister Theresa backed away from the building towards the gates surrounding the grounds. They were firmly closed. Panic overtook her. She couldn't be found here. She needed to call the police. Protect the babies. The only place she could hide was behind a small bush near the gates. She prayed that the people in the van would not notice her slipping out when they returned. Just above her a bright spotlight shone towards the gates. Picking up a rock she threw it hard towards the light, smashing it, and everything went dark. She waited, shaken and nauseous.

As the van revved past her, Sister Theresa waited until the last minute to run through the gap between the gates. Her heart raced as she recovered her bicycle and threw her feet onto the pedals. A single gunshot rang out, behind her, filling her with fear and dread. It was downhill to the convent, but she still pedalled as fast as her shaky legs could manage.

As Sister Theresa arrived at the back door to the convent, she heard the distant rumble of a car. She ran to the nursery and burst in, frightening Sister Mary with her uncharacteristic noise.

"The babies. They need to be returned to the sea. I'm calling the police. Please believe me. They're coming for them. It's the only way to save them." She waited only long enough to register the nod from Sister Mary before running to the phone. Picking up the receiver she listened for the dial tone. Nothing. The telephone lines weren't working. There wasn't time. The men banged on the door, demanding to be let in.

She had to make a choice, save the babies, or report the Pisces Institute. She returned to the nursery to find Sister Mary and half of the babies gone, along with one of the prams. She bundled the rest into her arms, cramming them into the remaining pram, then ran towards the secret door at the back of the convent. For just a moment she was thankful that the babies weren't normal, their silence might just keep them all safe.

At the beachside, she found Sister Mary unwrapping her babies and releasing them into the sea. Each of them dipped underneath the water, then resurfaced, swimming comfortably. They released all the babies before the first gunshots rang out.

"Swim little ones," Sister Theresa said, urging the last few babies away from the shore. The beach was covered in men in dark clothing, holding weapons, encircling the two nuns. They clasped hands and backed into the water, dipping low as it got deeper.

"Can you swim?" asked Sister Mary.

"No. Can you?"

"No."

"Lord I pray for you to spare the children. Take them safely out to sea, and protect them from those who mean them harm," Sister Theresa said.

They both took a step deeper, out of their depth and felt the ground slip away beneath their feet. Bullets skittered across the surface of the water as they felt their bodies float free before being grasped by gentle, small hands. The babies' hands wrapped around their arms and legs, pulling at their clothing and pushing to keep their heads above water as they dragged them away from the beach.

Instead of the repulsion she had previously felt at the babies' touch, Sister Theresa felt a sense of peace and acceptance. The sounds of the guns faded as they drifted, rounding the headland to the beach beyond. Safe. Thank God. She caressed a silver-scaled cheek.

"Thank you."

These babies should never have been made, but unlike those who had produced them, they weren't evil. She felt with certainty that the Lord loved them just the way they were.

About the Author:

Carolyn Young is a single mum living in Melbourne with her children and rescue cats. Most of her writing falls under the speculative fiction banner with Young Adult dystopian as her main focus. She has several short stories appearing in both Australian and international publications.

A considerable amount of her life has been spent moving from one university course to another trying to find her place in the world before realising her interest in reading extended to an even stronger passion for writing.

She now spends her spare time reading, writing and dreaming of the day she can move to the country and write full-time.

As a writer she credits any and all success to her cat, who always knows the right keys to walk over to inspire creativity.

Carolyn's short story, 'The Beginning of the End' *was published in Aussie Speculative Fiction's anthology,* '**Beginnings.**'

Follow Carolyn at
www.facebook.com/authorcarolynyoung.

SEAMARE

Nikky Lee

12:00am February 18, 1961.

A flash of scales and he was falling, spiralling, spinning down. Down, down, into oblivion.

Captain Sanders woke to the scream of metal on rock and a smarting pain as his body thudded to the floor.

What in the—

A siren welled up from the deck, its crescendo drowning the shouts of his men. Sanders pulled himself up and groped in the dark, feeling along the wall for the switch. Found it. Yellow light flared from the lamp above, revealing his sorry state of a cabin. All four walls and floor were off-kilter, charts and papers scattered, his only photo of Maggie face down in a shattered picture frame.

The sight jarred in his head, and for a heartbeat he saw double. Or thought he did. He rubbed his eyes and the room snapped sharp again.

Sanders brushed off the glass, scooped out the photo and placed it into his breast pocket, and then reached for his shoes.

"What happened?" he demanded on entering the helm. "Did we hit something?" The moment he said it, he blinked, frowned, suddenly sure he'd said something like that before, long ago. Perhaps in a dream once.

The First Mate, Marin, beckoned Sanders over to the wheel. The man's face was pale, freckles livid on his cheeks and a sheen of sweat coated his forehead. "We're . . . run aground."

Aground? Sanders gawked, wondering if he'd heard right. He cleared his throat and managed to garble out, "Impossible, we're in open seas."

"I thought so too." Lines of worry wrinkled Marin's brow; an oddly familiar expression, but Sanders couldn't think when he'd seen it before. Marin rubbed a peephole into the fogged-up port window and pointed. "We should have clear sea for miles, but there's no arguing with *that.*"

Behind the glass, the floodlights from *The Oneiros'* helm flickered. For a heartbeat, her bow illuminated—thirty square feet of sloping deck and tangled rope. Fishing nets hopelessly matted. Below, jagged rocks crunched into the hull. Beyond, the cliffs of a headland lay. Land. Impossibly, undeniably, land. Then it was gone. Lost as the lights failed again and darkness flooded in.

"Shit." Sanders scrabbled to the forward window, rubbed another peephole. Too dark to make out how bad the damage was, but something in the way the ship flopped on the hidden reef said the keel was broken. Not good.

"Our radio's out too," Marin reported.

Sanders swore again. "Where the hell are we?"

"Not sure. Last reading said we were 217 miles off the Fox Islands. There shouldn't be anything here." Marin glanced at the instruments in the dash, then outside at the crippled vessel. A flash lit up the headland in the windows again, the sloping cavern of the cliff was a shade darker in the black and scarcely sixty feet off the port side. Sanders gut turned cold. It was a miracle they hadn't sailed headfirst into it.

Marin cleared his throat. "We're taking in a lot of water."

As if it'd heard him, the ship groaned: a deep, reverberating shudder that Sanders felt in his bones. Another spark of light. Water sluiced over the bulwarks, washing the deck in spray. Fishing buoys spun away in the swirl. The siren still blared.

Seas curse it. "Evacuate the crew. And find out where we Goddamn are."

Marin nodded, clamped a hand around the ship's PA and ushered the command. Men scampered across the deck, scurvy rats in orange overalls as they wrestled the lifeboats free from their holds.

Sanders watched them go. The summer night was unusually warm, hot and sticky, but at least his crew wouldn't die of cold. *Get them to shore, sort it out at daybreak.* Their cargo would survive a bit of flooding—as long as the hold wasn't breached. *A right pain if it was, after all that trouble catching her.*

He patted his shirt pocket, feeling the stiff photo paper flex under his touch. One last voyage. For Maggie. He glanced through the fogged glass at the hold, hatch still latched tight below on *The Oneiros'* deck. His last catch. With it, they'd finally have enough. Enough for Maggie's surgery. Enough to prove he wasn't an old sailor who'd traded his marbles for salt crystals. Enough for the white picket cottage he and Maggie had dreamed about for thirty years.

All he had to do was bring it—*her*—home.

Wind buffeted *The Oneiros,* bringing the stench of rotted fish with it. And something else. Sanders cocked his head.

"You hear that?"

Marin frowned. "You mean the singing?"

Sanders waved him off. "No, not that. She's been doing that since yesterday." He paused again, ears straining.

In the midst of pulling the emergency flares out from under the skipper's seat, Marin stopped and frowned. "Whistling?" He looked at the roof. "From above?"

They crowded against the portside window. Saunders wiped the condensation away with his sleeve. Another hot, sticky gust of wind buffeted the ship, teetering her like a broken seesaw on the reef. A prickle ran over Sanders; an echo of cold on his skin. He shuddered and felt for Maggie's photo again. *I'm coming home,* he promised.

He peered out through his peephole, waiting for the next flash of *The Oneiros'* floodlights. Then he saw it. Rocks above. Yellow rocks. Rocks with splinted wood and metal caught in them.

Sharp rocks honed to points; the wind howling between them.

Dear God. Sanders looked down. The reef lay below them, a matching jagged set. Not rocks.

Teeth.

The Oneiros groaned again, listing further onto her starboard edge. The helm tilted, pitching onto its side. Debris slid across the floor: a packet of smokes—Marin's probably; a navigation chart; a coffee cup. Sanders grappled for a hold, found it around the wheel and held himself steady. Marin slid with the rest of his possessions, thumping to a stop against the starboard porthole, his boots leaving imprints in the fogged glass.

Sanders squinted through the forward window. The impossible land lay ahead, wide and cavernous. Gullet open.

His men, just pin pricks of light on the water now, rowed towards it, paddles chopping at the water in their panic.

Turn back. He wanted to scream. *Go back. It's not—*

Too late. Already too late.

The jaws came down, the cavern closing upon the ship, ripping through metal and wire. Sanders closed his eyes, listening to the crunch of steel bones breaking. *The Oneiros'* lights went out. Water rushed in. Somewhere, Marin screamed.

And the singing stopped.

Sanders grip slipped on the wheel. The sea sucked him out, dragged him down. His body bounced off the rocks. Something shiny and sylph-like flashed in the dark water. Free.

Angry.

A cold hand coiled around his foot, fingers digging into flesh like teeth as she dragged him deeper. The black and white photo slipped from his pocket, fluttering in the gloom. *Maggie. Oh Maggie, I'm sorry.*

A face loomed close in the dim. Hairless, grey skin and orbs for eyes. Sanders screamed, bubbled and thrashed. She held him there, snared in her grip, as she had once been in his net. Sanders lungs burned; his head swam. She came close, displaying rows upon rows of teeth.

This is it.

He braced himself and waited for the end. Above, in his peripheral vision, bright scales flashed in the dark, darting through the murk. *Another one.* And there, a third glint of scales. *A school of them.*

Together the mermaids circled.

Round and round. Mesmerising. Yes, he'd felt this before—this sinking. This cold pressing on his skin. But it was too late. All of it too late. He was caught. Trapped in this cycle of scale and fin.

Saunders sank. His eyes slid shut. The last air in his lungs emptied.

Falling, spiraling, spinning down. Down, down, into oblivion—

12:00am February 18, 1962.
—And he woke to the scream of metal on rock and a smarting pain as his body thudded to the floor.

Up on the deck of *The Oneiros*, a siren wailed . . .

About the Author:

Nikky grew up as a barefoot 90s child in Perth, Western Australia, before moving to New Zealand in 2016. By day she works as a professional content writer and by night authors speculative fiction, often burning the candle at both ends to explore fantastic worlds, mine asteroids and meet wizards. Her creative work has appeared in magazines, on radio and in anthologies around the world. She is currently writing a dark fantasy trilogy, routinely sacrificing literary darlings to the editing gods in the hopes of seeing it published.

You can find her online at:
W:nikkythewriter.com | T:@NikkyMLee | F:nikkythewriter

THIS IS THE DAWNING (PART III)

Helena McAuley

The incarnation of the Grand Spirit of Pisces—Ruler of the Current Age and Guardian of the Fate of Humanity for the last two thousand years—lived in a California bungalow in the outer suburbs of the city. It had taken Doug and Capricorn a tram, a train, and a bus to get there, and now the sun was hanging low in the western sky, the heat of the day cooling. Capricorn had said *"space does not matter, only time matters"*, but space sure felt like a barrier when the trip took two and a half hours.

When Doug questioned this, Capricorn had told him *he* could unmanifest and be there in an instant, but that, until Doug incarnated as the Spirit of Aquarius, he would have to take the bus.

The flyscreen was locked, but the front door stood open to receive the breeze. Doug glimpsed a long hallway beyond, statues, wall-hangings, and salt lamps decorating its edges. He was waiting for Capricorn to knock, but the older man seemed uninclined to move. Doug made an impatient gesture and Capricorn's eyes flickered to him.

"It's unnecessary," Capricorn said, then tapped two fingers against his temple to illustrate his point.

Footsteps heralded the silhouette of a woman moving up the hallway towards them, and her large smile was visible through the screen door as she unlocked it.

"Aquarius!" she beamed in a voice throaty with emotion. She grasped Doug's hands and kissed him on each cheek. "It's been so long! How are you?"

"Unincarnate," Capricorn replied for him, his tone flat and bitter. "This is Douglas."

"Doug," Doug corrected.

"Well, Doug," Pisces said, and she pronounced it strangely, as if the simple name was foreign and exotic. "Blessings be upon you." She kissed his cheeks a second time. She repeated the gesture with Capricorn. "Blessings be upon you, too, my grumpy old Goat-fish."

Capricorn bristled at the pet name, and Doug snorted with laughter.

"Goat-fish?" he sniggered.

The responding look from Capricorn silenced him, but the warmth of Pisces' smile negated the tension. "Come in, come in—" she stood aside "—I have tea and biscuits."

"Ooo, biscuits!" Doug chirped; only just catching the warning shake of a head from Capricorn, though what the warning implied he couldn't fathom.

He found out soon enough.

The kitchen was quaint, the tea strong smelling, and the biscuits rock-hard. After nearly breaking his tooth, Doug set the unfinished biscuit back on the plate. Pisces didn't notice, releasing a contented sigh as she sipped from her dainty cup. Capricorn's own sat steaming before him—resolutely untouched. Doug lifted the ancient bone chinaware by the handle and took a tentative sip. He couldn't bring himself to swallow.

"It's good, isn't it?" Pisces enthused. "Dandelion and chamomile."

Doug discreetly let the liquid drain back into the cup.

Unperturbed, Pisces warmed her hands on her cup and deeply breathed the aroma. She was an average-looking woman; average height, average build, shoulder-length dark hair, streaked with grey and held back with a purple headband. But she was striking if only for her choice of decoration and personal adornment. Pisces was a walking embodiment of every new age cliché ever contrived; from her sea-green, wide-legged fisherman's pants, to the multicoloured robe of light fabric that hung from her frame, to the faint smell of incense that hung in the air. She had rings on her fingers, although Doug wasn't sure about bells on her toes, and around her neck on a leather thong was a polished but uncut aquamarine. He was uncertain if he should think of her as Pisces Incarnate, or Hippy Incarnate.

As if to illustrate the point, she opened her eyes and fixed them on Capricorn.

"Cap, what's the matter?" she asked, genuine concern in her voice. "You haven't touched your tea."

"I prefer the taste of coffee," Capricorn replied evenly.

Pisces gave a dismissive wave. "Oh, you won't find any of that poison here," she said. "Caffeine is stress distilled. This tea is soothing and relaxing, something I think you are desperately in need of at the moment."

Doug recalled the earthquake from earlier that evening, the pain and tension etched into Capricorn's face as he tried to quell the violence he had caused, and the warning cry from Pisces. The two sat before him as if locked in a battle of wills; Capricorn his ever-stern visage, Pisces empathic and indomitable, a well of calm compassion. Doug bowed his head between his shoulders in the growing tension and sipped submissively at his tea.

"Come on," Pisces said to Doug, breaking eye contact with Capricorn and turning towards him. "Let's have a look at you."

She took both his hands in hers and sat staring into his eyes, a beatific smile touching her lips. As Capricorn had done when they'd first met, she seemed not to be staring at him, but *into* him, *through* him. Searching not his face, but some internal realm.

"Ah, there you are," she sighed, the smile lighting her eyes. "Aquarius, welcome home."

Doug withdrew his hands, his cheeks burning from her familiarity and affection.

"What's so special about Aquarius, anyway?" he asked, lifting his tea to give his hands a distraction. "Why do you guys want him so much?"

"Oh, Doug, we want *you*. You *are* Aquarius," Pisces said.

"So Capricorn keeps telling me," and he was unable to keep the self-deprecation from his voice.

Pisces smiled, as if his personal flaws were beautiful in their own right. "Aquarius in and of himself is not any more special than the rest of us," she said. "But the *Age* of Aquarius is the culmination of our work. For millennia, with the coming of each Dawning, we contested and fought. It was Capricorn who suggested there was a better way. Our previous procession was disordered, chaotic, and it almost lead the Earth into chaos also. Capricorn gathered us and suggested there should be *order*, each Age building on the last to lead humanity towards the ultimate goal. Towards the ability to incarnate and dis-incarnate at will; just as *we* do. For humans to become beings of spiritual *and* material, form. Just as *we* are. Initially we all agreed. Since that time, though, the plan had its detractors, and so the battles continue, each Dawning. We have been the majority and have been able to maintain the order, but we've never been in a position before where the rightful ruler of the next Age has not been actively incarnate. And, of course, without Gemini . . ."

Doug felt a coldness rising in his chest. "What about Gemini?"

"She was murdered."

All eyes turned to Capricorn, but he seemed disinclined to say more.

Doug frowned, "I thought you guys couldn't die?"

"*We* cannot die," Pisces corrected him. "But our physical forms can cease to live, if we so let them. Or if another of the Twelve takes measures enough to end our form. You see, incarnation is not our natural state. It's burdensome, harrowing. Our minds were not designed to be encased in this material form; not forever." It seemed she was resisting the urge to glance at Capricorn. "We need time to rest, to gather our strength and regain perspective. The longer one is in the material world, the less that mind can connect to the world of the spiritual. That is how the battles started; we each remained incarnate for too long, we lost sight of our duty."

Capricorn stood and left without a word, exiting the sliding door that opened into the lush garden at the back of the house.

Doug's eyes followed him, but he remained seated.

Pisces' smile was at once loving and sorrowful. "The burden has rested most heavily on him," she murmured.

Doug tore his eyes from the image of the man standing in the fading light. "How so?"

"Capricorn has taken the responsibility for the human race upon himself," Pisces said. "He feels a sense of desperation that, I must admit, the rest of us do not."

"What do you feel?"

Pisces' reply was delivered in the form of a smile. "Love. Love should always be the first response," she continued. "Love is the means by which it is okay to fail, because failure is as much an act of achievement as success. It is love for humanity that must guide our actions."

"Are you suggesting Capricorn doesn't 'love' humanity?"

Her smile disappeared, leaving behind a look of uncertainty and hesitation. "Capricorn serves humanity," she said cautiously. "His dedication and obligation to this race is unquestionable." Her eyes turned to the man in the garden, and Doug's followed. "He feels the responsibility, and the burden that implies. But . . ." She bit her lip, and her eyes creased with sorrow. "I don't know if he remembers how to feel love . . ."

Doug watched Capricorn, who stood in the garden, head bowed. *'Please don't tell me I have wasted all that time'* had been the words, born from his lips in a moment of fear and uncertainty. He had said that space does not matter; only *time* matters.

And he had said he had been incarnate for a very long time.

Just how long? And what toll had it exacted from him?

Doug felt a sudden—and surprising—swell of pity for Capricorn. If these last few hours were an anime, Capricorn would be the 'mentor', and it would be a common trope that Doug would have unswerving loyalty for the preternatural being that suddenly changed his life. But real life didn't work like that. Did it?

It could. And it would. Capricorn had also said that all things were *choice*. And so Doug would choose to make it so. He saw their roles clearly; Capricorn, the mentor, a man—

albeit, a ridiculously OverPowered man of supernatural origins, but a man nonetheless—who was lonely, trapped in self-imposed isolation; not just skeletons, but demons in his closet. And Doug, the apprentice, the boy, who would learn from and support his mentor, and—if the fates allowed—would bring him some measure of salvation.

"Come on." Pisces' sorrow dispelled and her blithe nature returned. "We should get started."

"Started on what?"

Pisces laughed; a high, light laugh like a bell. "On getting you to incarnate, of course."

"Oh," Doug said. He grimaced. "I was worried you were going to say something like that . . ."

Do they think I cannot hear them? Has Pisces forgotten how manifestation works? I may be restrained to physical form, but that still does not make me a man. The senses are unrestricted, and I can hear every word.

"I don't know if he remembers how to feel love . . ."

Do I? Did I ever know? Does it even matter? No. I don't think it does.

I turn to the sky, and with sight that is as unrestricted as my hearing I see past the brightness brought by the sun, past the obscure haze of the atmosphere, and out into the beyond. I see the constellation that bares my name, thought by some of my fellows to be the 'true body'. I know that is not what it is. It is the resting place for the mind. At times I have inhabited it, taken refuge there, and watched the Earth turn in its cosmic dance—sometimes towards enlightenment, sometimes towards destruction.

Yes, I feel the responsibility. I feel the burden. But only because sometimes it feels that I am the only one who *cares.*

And they say I have forgotten how to love.

I close my eyes and feel the air's vibration for the Dawning, the surge in energy at its coming, the excitement of the particles of the physical world. Despite what many think, the Dawning is not a time. Nor is it a place. It is not made of anything belonging to the material realm. The Dawning is a state of mind, or, rather, a state of *minds.* It is an act of the conscious and unconscious will of humankind telling the universe that they are ready for *change.* Humans have calculated that the Dawning—the turning of one Age into another—occurs roughly every 2160 years, and they are correct in this. But it has nothing to do with how long it takes for the constellations to turn about the cosmos. It is only because this is roughly the length of time humanity *needs* in order to learn the lessons an Age can teach. That is why the precise moment of the Dawning is so difficult to define; it can take centuries to come, but then happen in an instant.

Humanity is so ignorant of the effect they have on the physical realm.

I tear my eyes from the sky and shake my head. I draw a deep breath, tasting the green of the trees, then I return to the house.

Pisces and Aquarius are sitting on the floor, deep in some kind of meditation. I raise an eyebrow at the ridiculous sight, but say nothing. Aquarius' chest swells with breath and, as if on the verge of ecstasy, he sighs.

"I am transformed!"

Nothing happens.

I frown. "What the hell was that?"

"Wait," he says, "I don't think that was right . . . Errr . . . Aquarius Powers! Activate!" Still nothing. He pumps a fist in the air. "Zodi-Cats, Ho!" When there is still no change he raises his fist higher. "By the Power of Aqua-Skull!"

This is just getting embarrassing, and I can tell from his bearing that he knows it.

"Moon Crystal Power make-up?" he sheepishly mutters.

No, not Aquarius. Only Douglas.

"Maybe meditation was not the best choice," Pisces reassures him, resting one hand on his knee. "Perhaps we would do better with some physical prompts."

I remain out of their path as Pi makes Douglas face the wall. I know where this is going. I hold my face in my hand.

"The ability to unmanifest is one of the most basic," Pisces tells him. "If you can achieve this, then remembering yourself as Aquarius should be second nature." She indicates the wall in front of him. "Go on."

Douglas shakes his head. "Go on what?"

"Try to pass through the wall."

It takes all of my will to resist the urge to turn away. Douglas first presses his hands against the plaster, then sets what little muscle he has behind it and pushes. I sigh and shake my head. Of course this was not going to work.

"Ninety per cent of all solid matter is the space between atoms," Pi tells him.

"Yeah, I've heard that," Douglas replies.

Pisces brightens. "Then this should be easy for you." She illustrates the point by stepping through the wall, the illusory barrier swallowing her visage, before stepping back again.

Douglas' eyes betray his confidence. "Yeah. Sure. Piece of cake." He interlaces his fingers before him and stretches his arms out, eliciting a cracking sound. "Okay, comrades, stand back."

"Pi," I say warningly.

Douglas takes a step back and his muscles tense.

"Oh God," I groan.

He strikes the wall full force, ricochets off, and falls backwards onto the floor, sprawling in an undignified manner.

I close my eyes and moan. I could've told them that was going to happen.

Pisces picks him up off the floor. "You've got to take it easy, Doug. Until you incarnate you could do yourself some serious damage."

"Pi, this isn't going to work," I tell her.

"Hush, you," she replies. "Have some confidence in the poor boy."

"Incarnation should be immediate. It's not something you work up to, it's something that simply *is*. There's obviously some kind of blockage in his brain. A reason why he won't *be* who he's supposed to *be*." I fix Douglas with a hard stare. "What is wrong with you?"

He's rubbing at his jaw. "Geez, now you just sound like my dad."

I open my mouth to reply, but that is when I hear it—a scream; coming not from without, but from within.

Pisces hears it, too. But what is surprising is so does Aquarius. He grasps at the sides of his head with a cry of pain and doubles over. Pisces holds him by both forearms, keeping him upright.

"Doug! It's okay, try to filter it out."

"Oh *God!* My brain is on *fire!*"

While they're messing around, I'm busy trying to locate the scream. It feels close. It feels *familiar.*

Help me! Oh, please, God, somebody HELP ME!

"It's one of ours," I say.

"But they're not incarnate," Pisces replies while Douglas dissolves into sobs. "Another one? I thought there was only Aquarius!"

The presence is familiar to me, but not enough to spark recognition.

Douglas lets out a pathetic shriek.

"Stay with it," I order him. "Hold it in your mind. *Feel* what they're trying to tell you."

His breath comes in rapid gasps, but he seems calmer. He looks up and his wide eyes meet mine. "It's a girl . . ."

I nod. That's enough for now.

PLEASE! the cry comes. *She's going to KILL ME!*

"We have to help her!" Douglas shouts.

"And we will," I assure him. I turn to Pisces. "Can you find the source?"

Her eyes are glazed for only a moment. "Bicentennial Park," she says, shocked. "That's only a few blocks from here."

I chortle. "Well, what are the odds? Come on," and I grasp Douglas' arm. "You're going to get your first taste of battle."

To be continued in the next edition of the Zodiac Series— *Aries . . .*

About the Author:

Helena McAuley once mistook Vegemite for Nutella. It didn't end well.

When not writing or making dubious culinary choices, McAuley can be found contemplating her navel and the stars, and, in both instances, she wonders how so much dust has wound up there.

'This is the Dawning' is a serialised debut that will be published throughout the ASF Zodiac series. Who could be calling out to Doug and Cap? The answer is probably obvious, but maybe check it out anyway?

She can be found twit-ing, insta-ing, and occasionally facebooked under the handle @thathmc

Fun Fact: Pisces is often considered to be the tastiest sign of the Western Zodiac, especially when paired with pasta and a Napoli sauce (note: not a real fact, just an opinion).

ABOUT AUSSIE SPECULATIVE FICTION

Aussie Speculative Fiction is a recently established group which was created to support and promote Australian speculative fiction writers.

Check out our links:

www.facebook.com/Aussiespeculativefiction/

www.twitter.com/aussiefiction

www.aussiespeculativefiction.com

www.books2read.com/rl/asf

ABOUT DEADSET PRESS

Deadset Press is the publishing imprint of Aussie Speculative Fiction—a community aimed at supporting Australian and Kiwi authors. You can learn more at:

www.aussiespeculativefiction.com

ALSO BY DEADSET PRESS

<u>Annual Anthologies</u>

Beginnings: Aussie Speculative Fiction Anthology Vol. 1

Journeys: Aussie Speculative Fiction Anthology Vol. 2

Revolutions: Aussie Speculative Fiction Anthology Vol. 3

<u>Drowned Earth</u>

Prequel: Shards of Silver by Alanah Andrews

The Rise by Sue-Ellen Pashley

Fire Over Troubled Water by Nick Marone

Submerged City by Austin P. Sheehan

Tides of War by Marcus Turner

The Jindabyne Secret by Jo Hart

River of Diamonds by S. M. Isaac

Salvaged by C.A. Clark

Emoto's Promise by Shel Calopa

<u>Charity Anthologies</u>

Stories of Hope

Stories of Survival

<u>The Zodiac Series</u>

Capricorn (The Zodiac Series #1)

Aquarius (The Zodiac Series #2)

Pisces (The Zodiac Series #3)

Aries (The Zodiac Series #4)

Taurus (The Zodiac Series #5)

Gemini (The Zodiac Series #6)

Cancer (The Zodiac Series #7)

Leo (The Zodiac Series #8)

Virgo (The Zodiac Series #9)

Libra (The Zodiac Series #10)

Scorpio (The Zodiac Series #11)

Sagittarius (The Zodiac Series #12)

www.ingramcontent.com/pod-product-compliance
Lightning Source LLC
Chambersburg PA
CBHW020151120726
47903CB00007B/2498